Linus closed h
collapsed aga

That might have been one of most difficult things he had ever done. *Give yourself a pat on the back, old boy. You behaved like a gentleman.* Eighteen months ago, if a beautiful woman threw herself in his arms, he would have kissed the daylights out of her. Lips that soft and delicious? How could he resist?

But he did resist. Had to. It was clear his neighbor needed a friend far more than she needed sex.

I need to prove I'm not a disappointment.

How could the woman with whom he'd spent the evening disappoint anyone? It was inconceivable. She was funny. Beautiful. Smart.

Still, he'd done the right thing. Maybe that meant he was evolving into a better person. Because for once he cared more about helping a woman than seducing her.

Now, if only he could stop thinking about how amazing Stella's lips tasted, he'd be fine.

Dear Reader,

If you've been reading my Christmas stories, then you're already familiar with the Collier family.

I confess this book's hero, Linus, is my favorite Collier sibling. The seemingly carefree one who's advised both his brother and sister in ways of the heart. But behind his smile lies a guilt-ridden conscience.

Stella Russo is exactly the woman he needs in his life. She's in the middle of an identity crisis, caught between family expectations and her own desires. I'm not going to lie—a lot of her personality was inspired by my own personal struggles.

Circumstances make them neighbors. Chemistry will make them lovers. The question is, will their love affair last?

There's also a very funny backstory regarding this story. About a year ago, I jokingly told my unconvinced editor I was going to write about a millionaire cat.

Never tell a writer an idea sounds implausible. That's like handing us chocolate and telling us not to eat it. I replied with two words, "Challenge Accepted." The result was Etonia Toffee-Pudding—Stella's "employer."

I hope you enjoy this story. It's a little different, but I hope just as romantic. Drop me a line at Barbara@barbarawallace.com and let me know.

Barbara Wallace

A Year with the Millionaire Next Door

Barbara Wallace

Recycling programs
for this product may
not exist in your area.

ISBN-13: 978-1-335-55640-0

A Year with the Millionaire Next Door

Copyright © 2020 by Barbara Wallace

For questions and comments about the quality of this book,
please contact us at CustomerService@Harlequin.com.

Harlequin Enterprises ULC
22 Adelaide St. West, 40th Floor
Toronto, Ontario M5H 4E3, Canada
www.Harlequin.com

Printed in U.S.A.

Barbara Wallace can't remember when she wasn't dreaming up love stories in her head, so writing romances for Harlequin Romance is a dream come true. Happily married to her own Prince Charming, she lives in New England with a house full of empty-nest animals. Occasionally her son comes home, as well! To stay up-to-date on Barbara's news and releases, sign up for her newsletter at barbarawallace.com.

Books by Barbara Wallace

Harlequin Romance

Destination Brides

One Night in Provence

The Men Who Make Christmas

Christmas with Her Millionaire Boss

Royal House of Corinthia

Christmas Baby for the Princess
Winter Wedding for the Prince

The Vineyards of Calanetti

Saved by the CEO

In Love with the Boss

A Millionaire for Cinderella
Beauty & Her Billionaire Boss

Their Christmas Miracle
Her Convenient Christmas Date

Visit the Author Profile page
at Harlequin.com for more titles.

**Praise for
Barbara Wallace**

"I've read many of this author's works and this is definitely one that I enjoyed the most! This romantic story included some unexpected twists that had me hooked from the beginning to the very sweet conclusion. This one is a keeper to be read over and over!"

—*Goodreads* on *Their Christmas Miracle*

PROLOGUE

Actress Leaves Fortune to Pet!

Dame Agnes Moreland, who passed away last month, left her entire estate, solicitors have revealed, to Etonia Toffee Pudding—a ten-year-old pedigreed Turkish Angora.

The cat was listed as the sole recipient of Ms. Moreland's £11.2 million fortune. The funds are to be placed in an independently managed trust for the feline's care.

According to the terms of her will, Ms. Moreland's only living relative, her nephew, Theodore Moreland, of London, England, will inherit the remainder of the estate upon the cat's death.

Considered by many to be a grand dame of English theater, Agnes Moreland first gained recognition for her performance as Adelaide in Come the Night *in 1951.*

During her career she received countless honors and awards, leading to her receiving a DBE in 2012. In her later years she was known for her eccentricity, which included traveling with her pet.

An outside estate manager has been hired to care for the cat and manage the property.

CHAPTER ONE

Summer

STELLA STOOD ON the rooftop terrace and breathed in the warm summer air. Before her lay Belgravia, the London neighborhood whose stucco mansions and crescent-shaped streets once played home to Neville Chamberlain and Ian Fleming. Now she would walk in their footsteps.

She allowed herself a satisfied sigh. "Congratulations, Stella. You finally made it to the penthouse." And it only took a nervous breakdown to make it happen.

Her parents would say she was being overly dramatic. They preferred the term *burnout*, or better yet, no term at all, as if her freezing in midtown traffic had never happened.

Whatever the term—or lack thereof—she was here, in London, living in a luxury penthouse for the next twelve months. A pretty decent perk if she said so herself.

"What do you say, boss? Should we continue unpacking?" she asked.

Etonia Toffee Pudding lay across the top of a

bespoke velvet sofa as if she owned it—which she did. Until this morning, the Angora had been bunking with Peter Singh, the estate's attorney, and upon returning home, she had wasted no time reclaiming her space. She blanked her mismatched eyes in response to Stella's question.

"I'll take that as a yes." Stella adjusted the band that was keeping her hair out of her face. The chin-length bob was supposed to be low maintenance. Unfortunately, no one told her bangs were not.

Across the room, a portrait of Dame Agnes Moreland looked down from over the mantel, a sleepy-eyed smile playing on the late actress's lips as though she was laughing at a bunch of humans kowtowing to her pet.

"I may talk to her, but if you think I'm going to start carrying the animal around like you did, you're crazy," Stella said. Taking care of the cat was part of the job, same as managing the estate's property and investments. The cat wasn't a pet. "Right, kitty?"

A knock on the door interrupted the conversation. Sharp, loud raps that made Stella jump. "What the…?" The apartment occupied one half of the top floor and was accessible only by private elevator. The only other person up here would be her neighbor from across the hall.

The knocking continued. Etonia Toffee Pudding disappeared under the sofa fringe.

"I'm coming!" Stella called. If this was how the person planned to introduce themselves, it was going to be a long year.

Looking through the peephole, she saw a man in a tweed jacket. He had thinning gray hair and blotchy skin, the kind of complexion that came from spending too much time indoors. He didn't look like the kind of neighbor who popped in for a cup of coffee. If he even *was* her neighbor. To play things safe, she slid the door chain in place before opening it.

The man's eyes looked her up and down through the opening, clearly unimpressed with her cutoff shorts and Big Apple T-shirt. "My name is Theodore Moreland," he announced, the words reaching Stella on a waft of pungent mint. "Is the estate manager available?"

So, not the neighbor, but Dame Agnes's nephew. Peter had warned her about him.

"I'm the estate manager," she answered. "Stella Russo."

Moreland scowled. Stella tamped down the flutter of insecurity that always bothered her when facing disapproval.

His opinion doesn't mean anything, Stella. You're the one in charge.

Lessons from her childhood kicked in—when

in doubt, act as if you don't care—and she lifted her chin. "What can I do for you, Mr. Moreland?"

"To begin, you can open the door and let me inside," he said.

No, Stella didn't think so. At least not until she talked to Peter Singh. According to all accounts, Theodore Moreland had taken the terms of his aunt's will very poorly and was actively working to have the will declared invalid. Letting him inside would only invite disaster.

"I'm not really prepared to receive guests today," she told him. "I'm still unpacking and getting acquainted with my new boss."

"Are you refusing to let me enter my aunt's home?"

"You mean Etonia Toffee Pudding's home," she said, "and yes, I am."

Moreland's jowls flapped as he worked his jaw up and down. "How dare you. You have no right—"

"Actually, as the estate manager, I do. I'm in charge of all comings and goings, in fact." She made a mental note to talk to the downstairs security guard about calling before sending visitors upstairs. "Perhaps in a day or two, when I'm settled in, you and Peter can come by and we can talk."

Stella had never actually heard a man harrumph before. His mottled skin turned cranberry, calling attention to the veins crisscrossing his nose. The color reminded Stella of the drunks that used to sleep on the benches in central London. For that matter, so did the sheen in his eyes.

"Well, I never," he said in a minty huff. "I insist you let me in in this instance."

"I've already said no. You're going to have to come back next week." No longer feeling polite, she went to shut the door in his face, only to have him jam his foot between the door and frame.

Shoot.

"Is there a problem?" a voice asked.

"No," she and Moreland replied together.

A face appeared behind Moreland's shoulder. This one was far more attractive, with eyes the color of the Atlantic Ocean. The newcomer looked back and forth between them. "Causing trouble, Teddy?"

"This is none of your concern, Collier," Moreland replied.

"Mr. Moreland was just leaving," Stella added. "Weren't you, Mr. Moreland?"

"Is that why his foot's in the door?" the stranger asked.

"Agnes Moreland was my aunt. As her only living relative, it's my responsibility to make sure her property is managed soundly."

"Funny. I thought she asked that an estate manager be hired for that job. In fact, I distinctly remember that you weren't named caretaker."

Moreland's face grew redder. "This is none of your business."

"Au contraire, Teddy. I own half of this floor, which means you're causing a row on my property. That makes it very much my business. Now, Ms....?"

Stella smiled. "Russo. Stella Russo."

"Pleasure to meet you, Ms. Russo. Would you like Teddy, I mean, Mr. Moreland, to leave?"

"Yes, I would."

"There you have it, then. We would both like you to leave. Hopefully you will do so without further fuss. Otherwise, I might have to call security, and I don't think any of us want the unnecessary attention. Do we, Teddy?"

Moreland's caterpillar eyebrows merged together as he glared at the two of them. For a moment, Stella thought he might argue. In the end, however, common sense won out. "I'll be back," he said.

Stella couldn't wait.

Linus pretended to fiddle with his keys until Moreland stepped on the elevator. He would be back soon enough, asserting his rights as Agnes's nephew. "My nephew is nothing if not predictable," Dame Agnes used to say. That poor estate manager was going to have her hands full.

When the news first reported that she'd left her money to her cat, Linus was probably the only person in all of London who wasn't surprised. Dame Agnes spent her life being strong willed and eccentric. Why would anyone expect her to be different in death? When it came to finding someone to actually carry out Agnes's wishes, Linus assumed the law firm would hire some kind of professional cat lady. Someone older, who wore cardigan sweaters and pearls.

Shame on him, because from what he could see of his new neighbor, she wasn't old, and she definitely didn't wear cardigans. She had better legs than he'd imagined, too. He caught a glimpse of them—all right, he took a good look—before she shut the door. Those cutoff shorts were splendidly short. God bless current fashion.

Toeing his shoes off by the front door—Mrs. Paracha hated it when he walked on her clean floors in his dirty shoes—he picked them up and headed to his bedroom. He was halfway up the stairs when his phone began to chirp like a cricket.

He let it ring several times before answering. "Linus Collier speaking."

From the other end of the line came a loud

sigh. "Why do you insist on doing that?" his sister, Susan, asked.

"Doing what?"

"Answering so formally. We both know I'm the only person you have programmed to ring as a bloody cricket."

"Because." You could fill in the blank with a number of answers. Because it annoyed her. Because that was what big brothers did. Because he was supposed to be the quirky middle child and so it was expected. "Why are you calling me on a Friday night? Shouldn't you be out with your boyfriend?" he asked.

His sister was dating Lewis Montoya, the ex-footballer. The two of them made a rather odd couple, his prickly baby sister and the reformed Casanova, but they seemed to be making it work. Lewis's turnaround gave him hope that zebras could change their stripes.

"Movie night," Susan replied. "We're going to watch that rock-'n'-roll documentary everyone's talking about. Interested in joining us?"

A romantic Friday night playing third wheel? Sounded peachy.

Walking into his bedroom, he loosened his tie before lying down on the bed. "Thanks for the offer, but I've got plans."

"Really? What?"

Anything else, he almost answered.

"Nothing fancy. Dinner. Paperwork. A couple of pints."

"In other words, nothing."

And what was wrong with that? "I'll have you know Mrs. Paracha made her lamb stew. One doesn't walk away from such culinary perfection."

Another sigh. "Linus…"

"Susan…"

"I'm serious. What is going on?"

"I don't know what you're talking about."

"Yes, you do. You've been preoccupied and living like a monk for months. It's not like you."

Ah, but that was precisely the point. He was an outrageous flirt who hurt people without thinking. He wanted to be someone different. Someone better. "Maybe I'm on a journey of self-discovery," he told her.

"Are you? Or are you punishing yourself?"

"Must you attempt to ascribe a motive to everything?" He wasn't in the mood for her armchair psychology, especially when it cut close to the truth. "Maybe I've had a long day and feel like staying in. Is that so unbelievable a concept?"

Her silence spoke volumes.

"By the way, I met the new neighbor today," he said, changing the subject.

"The million-pound pet sitter? What are they like?"

"Antisocial. Teddy Moreland was on her doorstep."

"I'd be antisocial, too, under those circumstances. Did you see her? You did say she was female."

"Yes, she's female. American, from the sound of her accent."

"Huh," his sister said. "I wonder what would make someone cross the Atlantic to become a pet sitter."

"Giving a guess, I'd say it was because she likes cats and wants to live in London. There are worse ways to make a living."

Rather than answer, his sister let out an uncharacteristic half giggle, half squeal that left him rolling his eyes. Only one person made his sister giggle, and that was her boyfriend.

"Sorry," she said. "Lewis surprised me coming out of the shower."

"Is that what the kids are calling it these days?" In the background he could hear mumbling, followed by another giggle.

And they wondered why he didn't want to join them for movie night.

Seizing the opportunity, he wished his sister a good time and ended the call.

It was nice, he thought, as he stared at the ceiling, to see his siblings find happiness. Both Susan and their brother, Thomas, deserved it.

Someday maybe he'd again believe he did, too.

He continued to stare at the ceiling, but in his mind he saw his nightstand and the cream-colored envelope tucked inside. The letter had been neatly written, the lines painstakingly straight, each cursive loop the same height and width. Perfect penmanship to deliver a harsh truth.

It wasn't the first swipe at his behavior. Just the first one to hit home. The first one to make him truly understand the consequences of being Linus Collier, playboy.

Better to live like a monk until he learned to be someone else.

He lay on his bed until nature called too loudly to be ignored. Struggling to his feet, he made his way to the bathroom, barely registering the way the sun filtered through the terrace plants to cast shadows on the floor.

Until he heard the meow, that is. Forgetting all about nature, he looked out the terrace door and then down.

A large white cat with mismatched eyes looked back.

Stella stared at the stacks of cans in the pantry. Thirty of them, organized in groups of two by flavor. Chicken. Chicken and liver. Chicken and salmon. Chicken and tuna. Flavors were to rotate daily with no flavor repeating two days in a row. Apparently Etonia Toffee Pudding didn't like repetition. She did like chicken, though, because she was also to receive one chicken tender roasted fresh at midday. A note on the instruction file said that the housekeeper would take care of the cooking. The woman wouldn't be returning from leave, however, until tomorrow.

From down the hall, the grandfather clock chimed six times. Stella plucked a can at random and hoped it wasn't a duplicate.

"Dinnertime, kitty!" she called. *Etonia Toffee Pudding* was way too much of a mouthful.

Odd, but she assumed the cat would come running as soon as she peeled back the lid. Wasn't the sound supposed to be some kind of universal feline signal? Maybe British cats weren't as needy as American cats. She set the bowl on the floor.

Where was the cat? "Kitty?"

She headed down the glass-lined corridor, back to the living room. The velvet sofa and matching chairs were empty. No one was hiding underneath, either. "Here, kitty, kitty," Stella called. Where the dickens was she hiding?

Just then, the doorbell rang, causing her to jump. Again. So help her, if that was Theodore Moreland, she was going to slam the door on his foot.

It wasn't Teddy. It was her neighbor, the handsome one with twinkling eyes. He smiled and lifted a furry white face up to the space in the door. "Lose something?" he asked.

Stella stared at the animal in his arms. "Etonia?"

"She prefers Toffee," he replied.

Whatever. What was he doing with her?

"Found her meowing at my terrace door, asking to come in."

"But that's impossible. You're on the other side of the building." Except the terraces wrapped around the corners and she'd been standing in the opening when Teddy knocked. Stella looked over her shoulder at the terrace door.

"Dammit. I left the slider open when I went to let Mr. Moreland in. She must have run outside while we were talking."

"Smart cat. If only we could all escape from Teddy's visit."

"I'd rather she did her escaping under a bed," Stella said as she unlatched the door. "Come here, you naughty kitty." The cat let out an indignant meow at being transferred, but she settled down once Stella cradled her. "Thank you for bringing her back. I would have had a heart attack when I discovered her missing. You and I are going to have a long talk about house rules, missy," she said.

"She doesn't look too worried."

"Probably because she knows who's the boss

in this house. Come on inside. It's time for her supper, and I don't want to put her down while the door is open."

While her neighbor did as he was told, she set Etonia—or rather, Toffee—on the floor. The cat, having understood the word *supper*, immediately trotted toward the kitchen. "I wanted to..."

The words caught in her throat. For the first time, she got an unobscured view of her neighbor. Originally, she'd pegged him has handsome, but now that she had a better view, she realized that description was inadequate. Linus Collier was capital-*H* handsome. Tall and slender, he was built to wear his custom-made suit. His sandy-brown hair was stylishly cut and he had sharp features that gave him an aristocratic air. All and all, he looked exceedingly sophisticated and very British—if that was a thing. Standing there wearing a training camp T-shirt and tattered sneakers, Stella felt extremely common.

She coughed and started again. "I wanted to thank you for earlier. With Mr. Moreland."

"No need to thank me," he said, waving a hand. "You looked to have the situation well under control."

She liked to think she did, too. However, confirmation was nice to hear. "Even so, I appreciated the gesture. It was very gallant."

His laugh was sharp. Self-deprecating. "You

give me far too much credit. I was simply there for the entertainment value. Teddy's been making himself at home up here for as long as I can remember. He visited Agnes pretty much every week."

"Really?" And yet Dame Agnes had cut him from the will. Since she'd taken the job, Stella had been trying to ascertain why someone would skip over a relative in favor of a pet.

"I know what you're thinking," Linus said. "Do not mistake frequency with quality." Hands in his pockets, he strolled toward the glass wall. The late-afternoon sun caught the highlights in his hair, turning them golden. "Agnes left Teddy out of the will for good reason."

"Which was?"

"She liked the cat better," he said, turning and tossing a grin over his shoulder.

Stella grinned and looked away. The man had to know how attractive he looked doing that. If he didn't, then he was either clueless or his apartment lacked mirrors. "Did you know Dame Agnes well?"

"Well enough. Her last few years she began inviting me over for dinner, and we developed a friendship. She once made me read Othello to her Desdemona. Said practicing lines kept her mind sharp."

And having a handsome dinner companion probably kept her spirits up.

Just then, a sated Toffee came strolling down the hall. In a demonstration of superiority, she plopped herself down against Linus's leg and began washing her paw, completely unconcerned with whether she was getting hair on his pants or not.

"Do you think she knows she's worth the cost of a Van Gogh?" Stella asked.

"Oh, I'm fairly certain she thought herself priceless before Agnes passed. Isn't that right, you little diva?" Bending on one knee, he buried his fingers in the fur at the back of Toffee's head. The cat immediately began purring like a small engine. "Are you at loose ends now that Agnes is gone? Is that why you came hopping across to my balcony?"

He looked up, and Stella saw softness in his gaze that hadn't been there before. His eyes had become muted, shifting into a blue gray that reminded her of the sky right before the dawn. The change suggested there were layers to the man. That if you peeled back the charm and the good looks, you would discover something even better.

Of course, she wasn't looking to discover anything, but it was nice to think her neighbor seemed decent. She coughed away the thought, and said, "Nothing personal, but I'm planning on her escape being a onetime event. I prefer not to think of her taking that leap more than once."

"Can't say that I blame you." Giving the cat one last rub behind the ears, her neighbor stood up and tucked his hands back into his pockets. "Now that the fugitive has been returned to custody, I should let you get back to your unpacking. It was a pleasure meeting you, Ms. Russo. I hope…" The sentence drifted off, as if he thought better of whatever it was he intended to say. "I'm sure we'll run into one another again."

Stella was sure they would, too. Hard to avoid when they lived across the hall from one another. She walked him to the door, thanked him again for bringing home Toffee and said good-night. It wasn't until she locked the door that she wondered about the sentence he didn't finish.

CHAPTER TWO

A FEW DAYS LATER, Stella found herself working outside, the penthouse terrace being nothing like her tiny balcony in New York. The wraparound exterior had been designed with both sunrise and sunset views in mind, depending upon your location. The sunrise seats were off the dining room, while sunset was a few feet from the master bedroom. Agnes—or someone—had designed the space to flow accordingly. A breakfast table and a chaise lounge led to an outdoor seating area, which in turn led to a cozy love seat from which to enjoy the day's end. Like the apartment itself, the furnishings had a vintage elegance. Given her taste, Stella wondered why Dame Agnes had chosen such a contemporary apartment in the first place instead of one of the mansions a few streets over. Unless she liked being a study in opposites.

The lives of other people, their quirks and personal histories, had always intrigued Stella. When she was younger, before she focused on more practical subjects like finance and economics, she used to love to devour biographies of the important and famous, fascinated by the way their lives had played out against world history. Dame Agnes was precisely the type of person she found interesting.

On the chair beside her, Toffee stretched and rolled onto her back, a paw bent across her eyes. The cat had fought the leash and harness at first, but it appeared she was getting used to the idea. Beat being stuck inside or plunging to her death jumping off the terrace wall.

The thought of Toffee falling caused Stella to look next door. Her breakfast nook faced Linus Collier's sunset side. Only a few feet separated their terraces. When Stella first noticed, she could see how an enterprising cat might be tempted to make the jump. The thought made her nauseous. She wondered if Toffee hadn't seen a bird or something, and that was the reason she'd leaped. Linus had a trio of potted trees arranged in the corner. The plants partially obscured her view of what looked like more potted plants. He had a mile-high arboretum. For a cat, it would be temptation extraordinaire.

To Stella, the unexpected garden proved people were multifaceted.

She hadn't seen her neighbor since the day he brought Toffee home. Not that she was disappointed. She'd expected as much. People had lives. Jobs. Linus Collier probably had a very rich social life.

"What do you think he does for a living?" she asked Toffee. "Professor? Investment banker?" Both seemed too stodgy. "Member of the royal family?" He did give off an old-money kind of vibe. Plus, she could see him playing an old-money sport like polo.

"I know, I know," she said to Toffee's uninterested face. "Speculating about the neighbor isn't going to get my work done."

She turned her attention to the file in front of her. It contained a listing of the various properties and items of value that made up Agnes's— that was, Toffee's—estate. Her task over the next few days was to account for every piece of memorabilia and jewelry listed. Hardly high-level finance, but part of the job. Judging from the thickness of the file, there was a lot of memorabilia and jewelry.

She opened the first page and shook her head. Turned out Dame Agnes had included not only photos but background information. The top page read, "Sterling silver salt dishes from India, given by the Sultan of Brunei in 1959. We had dinner in his suite, and I complained that the curry was bland." The anecdote continued for several paragraphs.

"Oh, my," she said to Toffee. "This is going to be fun."

Before she could read any farther, however, the

alarm on her cell phone rang, letting her know it was midmorning in the States, the time when her father usually took a quick coffee break.

Kevin Russo answered on the second ring. "Hey, Dad," Stella greeted.

"Stella? Is that you? What are you calling for?"

His questions always sounded like she'd made a mistake. Stella did her best to not let the tone get to her. It was just his way, she always told herself. He didn't mean to sound accusatory. "You weren't home when I called the other night. I thought I'd call back to say hi."

"You're going to have to speak up. Wherever you are has horrible service."

"Hold on." She gave Toffee a quick glance before walking over to the front railing. "Is this better?" she asked, raising her voice a little.

"A little. Where are you?"

"On my terrace. Getting a little fresh air. It's a gorgeous day."

"Sounds nice," her father replied. "We got a delivery of oranges this afternoon. Whole place smells like Florida. You arrived in London okay, then?"

"Yeah. I'm all settled in."

"Well, that's good." Her father didn't hide the fact he disapproved of her taking a leave of absence, or "running off to Europe," as he put it. The Russos had left Europe so they could make something of themselves, he reminded her. Stella would lose career momentum. "You don't see your brother or sister needing a break from their stress, do you?" he'd said.

Back in the present, he remained awkwardly silent on the other end of the line.

"I started work this morning," Stella said. She started explaining about Dame Agnes's descriptions.

"Doesn't sound like finance," her father said.

"Can't manage an estate until I know what's included."

"I don't know. Sounds more like they're taking advantage of you. First making you watch that foolish cat, and now counting spoons or some nonsense?"

"I told you before, Dad, that foolish cat is my client. Watching her is part of the job. Did Mom tell you I'm living in a penthouse?"

"She told me," her father replied. "Sounds fancy."

"It is. I've got a housekeeper, too." Mrs. Churchill, who had worked for Dame Agnes, was in the house dusting.

"That's all great, but I doubt Mitchum, Baker is going to care much about your living arrangements. They're going to want you to have done more than pet sit for a year. If you want to catch up with your colleagues."

Stella closed her eyes. *It's just his way.* She wanted to tell him that Mitchum, Baker only cared that she did not freak out on their time. What she did on her leave was her business. But she didn't. For all his harshness, Kevin Russo wanted the best for his children. Wanted them to have success in a way that he hadn't. It wasn't his fault that Stella couldn't keep up with her siblings.

Nor was it his fault he couldn't understand Stella's decision, since she didn't completely understand it herself. All she knew was that her parents' option—that she spend a few weeks in Boston and then head back to work—made her struggle to breathe. It was like the very words *Boston, New York* and *Mitchum, Baker* squeezed the air from her lungs. The job posting in London was the first idea that didn't make her feel like she was having a heart attack.

"I'm résumé stacking," she told her father. Her voice sounded more defensive than she wanted. "When I return, I'll be one of the few risk-assessment managers with international estate-management experience. In today's job market, it's all about being unique."

"If you say so."

For a second, she might as well have been in Boston, with her father eyeballing her with his trademark doubt. Or was it her trademark doubt? He never looked at Camilla or Joseph with anything less than beaming pride. But then, she'd always been the less-than child. The one in the background. The one who wasn't quite as smart or as talented or as lauded as Camilla and Joe.

Pushing her hair back from her face, she changed the subject. "What's going on back home? Anything interesting?"

"Your brother won his case the other day. They're starting to talk about making him a partner. He'd be the youngest in firm history."

No surprise there. She leaned back against the wall and looked toward the apartment. Toffee was awake and had jumped on the breakfast table. Her little pink nose was sniffing the glass surface.

"And I haven't had a chance to talk with your sister yet. You know what it's like being a resident. Well, you can imagine."

Yes, thought Stella, she could. She could also imagine her sister sailing through the experience. Camilla was unflappable.

"She said she may present her latest study at a conference in Spain. I was telling Marjorie Bowman the other day that when Camilla's done with school, I'm going to have her work on my brain. See if she can make me smarter."

It was an old joke, one she'd heard before. Her father told either it or a variation to just about everyone he ran into. Camilla would make him smarter. Joseph would get him out of trouble. And Stella would count his money. At least that was the joke before London. He probably didn't say anything about her now.

When she returned, though… She would kick ass when she returned and show him—show the world, that is—that she was a force to be reckoned with at Mitchum, Baker.

She forced a smile into her voice. "I'm sure Mrs.…"

"Oh, for crying out loud. Don't stack them like that. You trying to bruise every orange in the crate? I've got to go," her father said. "I'm sorry, Stella, I've got to go. I'll talk to you later."

"All right," Stella said. "Love you."

Her father had already disconnected the call.

Stella set the phone on the ledge and let out a frustrated scream.

Linus loved his terrace. Over the last couple of years, he'd turned the balcony into a mini potted garden. His own high-rise nature retreat. If he was going to be alone with his thoughts, he might as well do so surrounded by flamingo trees and Australian bottlebrush.

This afternoon, having decided to work at home, he was lingering over a second cup of tea—one of the benefits of being part owner of the company. He had his bare legs stretched out in the sun while he caught up on Parliament's latest drama.

"Arrrgh!"

The cry cut through the city noise, making him start and nearly spill tea on his robe. There could only be one source at this altitude. Forgetting Parliament, he headed toward the western end of the terrace, where he spied his neighbor. She was only partially visible through the foliage, but it looked like she was pushing against the wall, her arms stiff and her hands wrapped around the metal guardrail. Unlike the other day, she was dressed for business in a purple sleeveless dress and, he hoped, high heels. Her hair wasn't pulled back today, either. It hung like a dark brown curtain in front of her cheeks.

In the old days of last year, he would have gone on an all-out charm offensive, hoping—planning, actually—to establish more than a neighborly friendship. After all, she had everything he liked in a woman: great legs and two X chromosomes. When it came to women, he didn't believe in being discriminatory.

"So long as they sleep with you, right?" his last ex-girlfriend had said.

She'd chosen to storm off before he could answer. Otherwise, he might have told her it was the challenge, not the sex, that mattered.

All that was before the letter. His new neighbor didn't realize it, but she was safe from his disreputable behavior.

Except here he was, watching her through the bushes like a voyeur. He stepped around the trees and into the open. "Are you trying to make the terrace wider?" he asked.

The question made her turn quickly. Her wide-eyed expression was made sensual by the parting of her lips. That the sensuality was unintentional made it that much more arousing. Linus willed himself to think dampening thoughts as he watched her recover. First straightening her back, then brushing the hair from her face.

"Didn't mean to startle you," he said, once she was finished. "I was reading the paper when I heard you scream. Is everything all right?"

"Oh, that." He could practically hear the blush creeping into her cheeks. "Frustrating phone call."

"I know how those go. Don't tell me work is already getting to you?"

"Not work."

Something else, then. He wondered what, but didn't ask. If his neighbor wanted him to know more, she would have said. "How is your charge doing today? No more flying leaps, I noticed." Leaning forward, he spied Toffee stretched out on a table. "Is that a harness?" he asked.

"We came to a compromise. She stays on the leash; I let her sleep outside while I work."

"Impressive. I'm surprised your arms aren't covered in cat scratches."

"She's surprisingly cooperative for a cat."

"Agnes did take her everywhere," Linus said. "She must have learned it was best not to put up a fight."

He studied the space between their respective ends of the terrace. The distance was no more than a few feet. Why had he never noticed how close the two balconies were to one another? Most likely because he seldom sat on this side. If he wanted to see the sunset, he repositioned the double chaise near the living room; the seat was far better for relaxing with company.

"I take it this is where she made her escape," he said, looking downward. Below he saw a small patch of green shrubbery.

"I still can't believe she did," Stella replied. "Something must have caught her attention in your garden. That's quite a display you've got going."

"Thank you. It's my way of bringing nature to central London."

"You mean other than the parks?" She pointed toward the Belgrave Square Garden grounds, which could be seen in the distance.

"Last time I checked, public parks frowned on

you having tea in your pajamas. This way I can enjoy nature on my terms. Not to mention that I find the different foliage inspiring."

"How so? Are you an artist?"

"I like to think there's artistry involved, but my brother would disagree."

She drew closer to her side of the wall. As she walked, Linus watched the way her hips rolled into her steps. Definitely high heels. Linus tightened the belt on his robe to keep his body from reacting.

"I'm a chemist," he said. "I'm head of research and development for Colliers of London."

"Oh, I've seen their products. They sell them at some of the high-end boutiques on Fifth Avenue. Sounds like a fun job."

"It has its moments." She hadn't made the connection yet. "At the moment I'm working on a new idea—scented oils and candles based on our botanical products. What do you think of a lavender-heather combination?"

"I don't know. I've never smelled heather."

"It's surprisingly floral. The problem is I can't decide on a top note. I want something clean but not too overpowering. Mint would be my first instinct, but there's also basil and...you're smiling." A tiny, amused smile. "Sorry," he said, rubbing the back of his neck. "I take the science of scents very seriously."

"Don't apologize. You love your job. That's nice."

"It's just that there are so many possibilities and combinations, I have trouble not getting carried away. My brother and sister are forever giving me a hard time."

"But isn't that what a scientist is supposed to do? See all the possibilities?"

"Will you do me a favor and explain that to my brother the next time he tries to rein in my research budget?"

"Sure. What is it about siblings that they feel the need to…"

The words died on her tongue. *Connection made.*

Stella cringed. Talk about clueless. He wasn't just the head of R & D. "Your family owns the company."

"Guilty as charged," he replied. "Although in fairness, Colliers is really my brother's company. I'm more of what you would call an active shareholder."

Six of one, half dozen of another. He still owned a stake in the company. Explained the penthouse, and the fact he was lounging about in his bathrobe on a weekday. "I can't believe I didn't make the connection," she said.

"Why should you?"

"Oh, I don't know, maybe because *your last name is Collier.*"

He laughed at her emphasis. "Personally, I'm glad you didn't. It was nice to meet someone who didn't know my history straight off. Meant we could get acquainted without pesky assumptions."

"Why would I assume anything?" Other than his being rich, which was fairly obvious seeing as how he lived in a penthouse apartment.

"When you have a famous name, people gossip. You never know what people may have heard. You know, rumors, preconceived notions and the like."

"I see." She didn't, not really, but the shadow that flickered across his face told her not to keep asking. She understood what it was like to be saddled with people's expectations, and their disappointment when you failed to measure up. "For what it's worth, the only assumption I had was that you could afford to live next door. Unless you're squatting and about to get tossed out."

"No squatting. At least not yet." It cheered Stella to see the light return to his eyes. Without their sparkle, his eyes—all of him, actually—lacked vitality. Like how a passing cloud marred a sunny day. She didn't know Linus Collier well, but he struck her as a man with a lot of life inside him.

Huh. Looked like she had made a few other assumptions.

"Speaking of jobs," he was saying, "we got sidetracked from our discussion. How is your job going? Beyond keeping Toffee in line."

"Haven't done a lot yet," she said. "At the moment, I'm conducting an inventory of the estate. Cross-checking items listed in the records, then listing what's appropriate for donation or auction, what should be saved for historical preservation, etc."

"A challenge, considering everything Agnes did in her career. Every once in a while, when I visited, she would trot out a photograph of her and some icon. Made me think she had boxes and boxes of memorabilia hidden away in one of the upstairs rooms."

"Based on the file Toffee is currently sleeping on, I think you may be right. I'm also going to be double-checking all the financial investments. Toffee has a very diversified portfolio. Between investments and properties…"

"Did you say *properties*, with an *S*?"

Sounded strange, Stella had to admit, especially when discussing a cat. "She owns two. This apartment and a country cottage in Berkshire."

"Really? Our family had a place in Berkshire. We had to sell it when my father died."

"I'm sorry." The apology was a reflex, born

out of a lifetime of etiquette lessons. Whenever someone mentioned death, you offered regrets.

Linus waved her off. "No need. None of us wanted to take the property on. Now that you mention it, though, Agnes often talked about going to the country. Your job will be to manage everything?"

"Yes and no. There's actually a team. My job is to take care of the day-to-day management, make recommendations regarding investments and, of course, make sure the heir is comfortable." When said like that, the job didn't sound all that awesome. "It's more challenging than it sounds."

"I'm sure it is," Linus replied. He leaned against the railing, causing the front of his paisley robe to gape. "May I ask you a personal question?" he asked.

"What?" She was busy trying not to stare at the freshly revealed patch of chest hair.

"What makes a person from America come all the way to London to take care of a cat's estate? Don't get me wrong—it's lovely to have you—but don't they have estates in your country?"

"They do." How did she explain her running across the ocean in a way that didn't make her sound unstable or weak? "But this job sounded interesting. I've never worked for a cat before or on an estate with such renown. And since I was looking to get away from New York for the next year—"

"Get away?"

Bad choice of words. "Travel bug. I never got my semester abroad, so I decided to come to London for the next twelve months."

"Your plan for seeing Europe. Smart."

"Oh, I won't be traveling. I'll be too busy working to see anything outside London proper. Except the summer house."

He was looking at her, confused. "I thought you said you had the travel bug."

"I meant to see London, not the rest of Europe. I figured I'd come, spend a year seeing the city, gain some invaluable experience in British finance and then head back to New York."

She could tell Linus didn't quite buy the story, despite it being true, minus the part about wanting to see London. Whatever. She wasn't about to explain. She didn't have time, even if she wanted to. A quick look at her phone said as much.

"Sorry to run on you," she said, "but I better get Toffee inside and brushed. Teddy Moreland wasn't kidding about contacting the law firm. He'll be here in fifteen minutes to provide me with some 'historical perspective' regarding my job."

"Lucky you. If he drones on too much, close your eyes and think of England."

Stella snorted. "I think that phrase is supposed to mean something else, but thank you for the advice. I'm planning to detox with a nice long run this afternoon."

"I had a feeling you were a runner. Your legs," he added. "You have runner's calves."

"Oh. Thank you." She guessed. Compliment or not, the idea Linus had checked out her legs closely enough to notice made her warm from the inside out. "I was going to pace out a route this afternoon when I was finished work."

"I usually go around 4:00 p.m. myself. There's a very nice route around the gardens in the park."

"Is there? I'll check it out."

"I tell you what," he said. "Why don't we head out together when you're done with your meeting and I'll show you."

"You… You want to go running together?"

"Why not? I'm going to run anyway. Unless you're one of those antisocial runners who only cares about besting her time. Are you?"

"Not usually." Running was something she did for health and vanity purposes only. Keeping track of times would only depress her, as they would invariably be less than her runner siblings.

"Then why not join me? I'll show you the best route, so you'll have the lay of the land for when you go the next time. Consider it a runner's courtesy."

"Sure," Stella replied. Why not, indeed? Wasn't as though the man was asking her on a date. Back home she joined male running friends all the time. Running with Linus would be no different.

Well, almost no different. Back home, when the guys invited her to run, she didn't get butterflies in her stomach.

CHAPTER THREE

WHAT WAS HE THINKING? Runner's courtesy, his behind. She was a grown woman, perfectly capable of using an online map. There was zero reason to volunteer to play tour guide. Except…

Something about the way she talked about herself made the nerves tingle. The self-deprecating comments—self-defeating, really—that she dropped into conversation. Her certainty she was about to be fired. When he spoke to her on the terrace, it was because he heard tears in her eyes. Over a bloody cat. Then there was a tension that emanated off her in waves.

Victoria had been uptight and self-deprecating, too. He thought it part of her charm. Considered it part of the challenge.

He'd missed the signs once. He'd be damned if he missed the signs a second time. And so, he was extending a friendly hand to his neighbor.

That's all. Just a friendly hand.

Idiot that he was, he should have thought about his ankle first. He knew when he rolled the damn thing the other day that he'd tweaked it, but he figured that between tape and adrenaline he would be fine.

Wrong. His foot throbbed, and they had another half kilometer before they reached Belgrave Square.

That'd teach him to be nice.

He looked sideways at his running partner. Stella wore earbuds, blocking any attempt at conversation. That didn't mean he couldn't treat himself to a look now and then. After all, he was embracing monkhood, not death. Her tank top and running shorts showed off her toned body to perfection.

It was funny. She had the body of an athlete, but she didn't move like one. He'd expected long, graceful strides that matched her legs. Instead, she was stiff jointed and awkward. She was someone who ran because it was good for her, but she was not a runner.

He tapped her on the arm. "Three more blocks and then turn left," he said. As though voicing the distance would make it feel shorter.

She nodded. All business.

That was another thing that bothered him. There were a few details missing from her answer about getting the job. Like why she decided to take a leave of absence from her usual job to become what was basically a glorified pet sitter.

She said she needed to "get away." Why? Had something—

The dip in the sidewalk came out of nowhere, causing his leg to collapse beneath him. He pitched forward, his hands and knees skidding across the concrete.

"Oh my God, are you all right?" Stella spun around the moment he went down. "What happened?"

"Bloody dip in the pavement." He rolled over onto his rear end. The entire situation was embarrassing. People were staring at him.

"Are you all right, mate?" one man stopped and asked. "Need a hand?"

Of course he wasn't all right. His palms were bruised and scratched, his knee had a raw red patch that would be stiff in the morning and his ankle was throbbing.

"I'm fine," he told the man. "No need to worry."

"Are you sure?" Stella asked. She crouched down to eye level, her eyes wide and very brown. Like melted chocolate. For a minute he lost himself in them.

"Linus?"

"Sorry. I'm all right. Nothing a stiff drink and an ice bag won't solve. Help me up?"

He didn't want a hand from the stranger, but he would take one from her. Her palm was moist from the heat. Oddly enough, he liked the feel.

Gripping her fingers tightly, he slowly made his way upright.

Only to come within inches of her concerned eyes again.

One of the things he'd learned over the years was that people had different body chemistries resulting in very different, very unique scents. Stella's scent, even with the musky undertones of exertion, was sweet. His body reacted with enthusiasm, arousal stirring deep inside.

"Thanks." He stepped back quickly, stumbling from the abruptness as well as the pain stabbing his ankle. "Dammit," he rasped.

"Is it your knee?"

"My ankle. I twisted it." So much for running. The last time he hurt his ankle, he didn't run for weeks. "I'm afraid I'm done for the day. You can go on, if you'd like. Three more blocks and turn left. You can't miss the park. It's large and very green." He took a step and winced on the word, killing his attempt at lightness.

"Nonsense," she said. "If I go on, how will you get home?" Before he could stop her, she had grabbed his arm to steady him. "We'll try walking back, and if that doesn't work, we'll flag a taxi."

"It's only a mild sprain, not a broken bone. I'll be fine. You don't need to hold me up."

"Are you sure?"

"Definitely." Besides, he didn't want to spend the next kilometer with her holding him. It felt too nice.

Slowly, the two of them made their way along the street. "I have to admit," Stella said. "Truncated run or not, the exercise felt good. Thank you for insisting I go."

"To be honest in return, you looked as though you could use the stress relief."

She laughed. "Whatever gave you that idea?"

"Your aggravated scream for starters." He'd practically wanted to hug her when she was berating herself. "Although I can't entirely blame you. I'd scream, too, if I had to spend a day with Teddy. How was it, by the way?"

"As you would expect. He made it very clear that he knew the house backward and forward. I got a complete tour. Then he made himself at home and proceeded to tell me how Dame Agnes changed her will when they had a spat, and that she had changed her mind since then."

"Couldn't have changed it too much since she kept the terms of the will."

"Oh, he knows. He claims Agnes had grown very forgetful in her later years. Not that he minds, according to him. He said his initial reaction was one of surprise, not anger. That he doesn't need the money, and it's not as if he won't inherit Agnes's estate after Toffee dies. Not that he wishes any harm to come to the poor sweet dear, of course."

Linus could hear Teddy droning every word. "Then he insisted on inspecting every room in the house to make sure everything was shipshape. This was after the tour, mind you. By the time he left, I was jonesing for a run like you wouldn't believe."

"I'm assuming 'jonesing' means you wanted one," Linus said. He liked the Americanism.

"Try dying for one," she replied. "Toffee had the best idea. She hid under the bed for the visit. Does he always drone on that way?"

"Do you mean like a pompous windbag? Usually. I do my best to avoid him. Was he drunk?"

"I'm not sure. His breath smelled like he'd swallowed a tube of toothpaste, so he's either got incredible dental hygiene or he was trying to mask something. Did I mention how much he loves Etonia Toffee Pudding? He insisted on using her full name every time. Says he's always adored her. I think he may be planning to challenge the will."

They stopped at a corner to wait for a traffic light. Linus lifted his foot to let his good leg bear the weight a moment. "What makes you think that?" he asked.

"Nothing specific. The way he kept talking about how much he loved Toffee made me think he was up to something. I don't know him very well, though. I could be mistaken."

Was she kidding? She'd captured him perfectly. "I wouldn't be surprised if he did mount a challenge. I was at the reading of the will. What he calls surprise certainly looked like outrage to me."

"What this meeting told me is that I need to be extra careful to have all my records in order so as to not give him any ammunition. I'm going to be the best feline caretaker in Europe."

"I'm sure Toffee will appreciate the dedication." Ahead, he saw a familiar blue and red sign and smiled. "Would you mind if we stopped at that restaurant?" he asked, pointing. "Mrs. Paracha doesn't work on Mondays, so I need to pick up some curry for supper." And give his foot a chance to rest. With the adrenaline having worn off, it was throbbing more than before.

Stella checked her watch. "If we hurry," she said. "Mrs. Churchill can only stay until 6:00 p.m."

Toffee was a cat, not a child; she'd survive a few minutes unsupervised. Linus kept the thought to himself. The comment wouldn't be well received. Not after her speech about being the "best feline caretaker in Europe."

"My stomach thanks you," he said instead.

They both bought takeout. Stella couldn't resist the aromas of turmeric and fresh-baked naan hanging in the air. Exercise always brought out the eater in her.

She watched Linus hobble the last few blocks. A bad ankle did nothing to take away from his gracefulness. He even limped elegantly. When they were running, it had taken all her effort not to keep watching him move. He ran with such fluid motion, like a natural athlete. Personally, she hated running, and only did so because she liked carbs.

She also liked how easy it was to talk with Linus. As they killed time waiting by sharing their days, she tried to remember the last time she had had such a relaxed conversation. Usually her brain ran amok, critiquing everything she said and did, but not with Linus. He made her feel comfortable with herself, at least in the present.

Maybe that was why, when they reached their homes, she invited him inside.

"I just thought it seemed silly to take our food into different houses to eat alone when we could eat together," she said when he hesitated.

For the first time in an hour, she second-guessed herself. Maybe he didn't find her company as relaxing as she found his. Or maybe he feared she was misinterpreting his kindness for something else. "But if you'd rather go home, that's fine. It's no skin off my nose either way."

"No," he replied. "It would be nice to eat across

from a real person instead of my television set. Lead the way."

Toffee was in the entryway meowing when she opened the door. Seeing the big fur ball safe and sound made her feel less guilty about being home five minutes late. There was a note from Mrs. Churchill on the entryway table.

"I hope she doesn't think I'm neglecting my job," she said while walking into the kitchen. The note said Toffee had had dinner, although you wouldn't know it. The crystal bowl was licked so clean it looked like it hadn't held food in the first place.

"Who? Mrs. Churchill? Why would she think that? Because you didn't arrive home when the clock struck six? I doubt she cares. Don't forget, the woman worked for Dame Agnes. I'm sure she's seen everything."

"Maybe, but I'm not Dame Agnes. Part of my job is to take care of the heiress here. Blowing off dinner doesn't look good."

"First of all, you didn't blow off dinner. You missed feeding time by…" He checked his watch. "Seven minutes. While I realize seven minutes is an eternity in cat time, it's not that huge a deal. If anything, after working for Agnes, Mrs. Churchill's probably relieved to see someone treating Toffee like a cat."

"You don't understand," she said, handing him a plate from the cupboard.

"Try me."

Maybe she was being overly conscientious, but she didn't want another failure on her résumé. What would people think—what would her family think—if she couldn't ace something as easy as taking care of a cat? "It's important I do this job right."

"Right or perfect?"

"Is there a difference?"

An odd look crossed Linus's face. Serious and intense, like he was seeing her for the first time. The expression left her feeling exposed. "You're thinking I'm an uptight nutjob, aren't you?"

"Did I say you were a nutjob? Oh good, we're in luck." Reaching over her head, he took a bottle from the wine rack. "I was hoping she had a bottle of Viognier left."

"Before you grab a corkscrew, let me check my inventory list." There were several collectible bottles listed. Her head would be on the block if they drank one.

"Doubt you'll find this label. I bought it around the corner myself for thirty quid. A wine snob Agnes was not. When push came to shove, the old broad stayed true to her coal-mining roots."

Without waiting for a yes or no, he took out the corkscrew. Stella watched as he handled the bottle with strong, capable hands. Everything he did, from running to scratching Toffee to changing the subject, he did deftly. She could see why Agnes had wanted his company.

"You and Dame Agnes were a lot closer than simply sharing dinners once in a while, weren't you?" she asked once her glass was poured.

"I told you, she liked my company. I flirted with her. Who doesn't like being flirted with?"

By a man who looked like Linus? No one. "It was kind of you to give her the time."

He shrugged. "She was a national icon. Hardly a sacrifice. Besides, it wasn't all one-sided. She listened to me a time or two as well."

"I'm surprised she didn't ask you to be Toffee's guardian."

"We discussed it, but I don't think she thought my lifestyle was cat friendly enough."

"Why is that? Did you own a dog?"

"No, I …" His features drew together as though he were weighing his next words. "Let's say I had an active social life until recently."

Meaning he didn't now? What happened? Something serious, she suspected, because his eyes had grown grayer. The color didn't suit.

"Does this mean I shouldn't worry about you throwing loud parties?" she asked.

"Not even a quiet party," he replied. "I'm on what you'd call a social sabbatical."

Stella assumed that was Brit-speak for sticking close to home. Again, she wondered why. Not that it was any of her business, but why would someone as handsome and charming as Linus need a break from his social life?

Afraid any further questions would look nosy, she sampled the wine instead. The label might not be expensive, but the dry taste went down smoothly. She took a large sip, savoring the metallic apricot flavor on her tongue, and let the remaining tension from the day ebb away.

"This is delicious. You have good taste."

"Thank you. I pride myself on being able to buy the best inexpensive wines in the city. I leave the high-end buying to my siblings. Scotch whiskey, on the other hand, is a different story. Give me a couple hours and I'll tell you everything you need to know."

"My father is all about buying expensive wine. The higher the price tag, the better. He and my mother took some kind of class, too, so they can use words like *bouquet* and *finish*."

"I had a stepmother who did that. Always sounded like too much work to me. Dining room or living room?"

"Living room. You can elevate your ankle. And that's a bold statement coming from a man who makes his living evaluating different scents."

"Different animal," he replied as he limped toward the sofa. "Chemistry is my job. Wine is a drink. I don't need to work that hard for my beverages."

"What about Scotch?" Didn't he say he'd talk her ear off on the subject?

"My dear girl, Scotch is nothing like wine. It's art in a glass."

"I stand corrected." The conversation was completely nonsensical, which only made her relax more.

Once Linus was seated, she set one of the pillows on the coffee table and insisted he rest his foot. Then, after making sure he didn't need an ice bag, she settled next to him. Toffee immediately jumped between them. With her head resting against Stella's thigh and her tail draped across Linus's, she began purring.

"Someone feels at home," Linus remarked.

Stella swallowed her mouthful of wine. "Maybe your company reminds her of the old routine."

"Maybe. Or she's accepted you."

"Or she decided this was the most comfortable spot in the room. Never underestimate a cat's ability to know the best place to sit." She raised her glass. "To cats and their uncanny knack for putting their comfort first."

Linus tapped his glass to hers. "And to neighbors who help you limp home," he said. "Appreciate the helping hand."

"Don't sweat it. That's what friends are for, right?"

His eyes widened. "You consider me a friend?"

"Shouldn't I?"

He looked into his glass for a moment before looking back at her and smiling. "Yes, you should." As she met his gaze with a smile of her own, Stella felt a ribbon of satisfaction winding through her. The feeling reminded her of how she felt those times when—if—she did something right and made her parents proud. At the same time, the feeling was different, too. Her parents' pride never made her insides turn upside down. Suddenly she realized why.

This sensation wasn't satisfaction—it was pleasure.

"Do you find it difficult, being the spare?" Dinner was over and they were enjoying the last of the wine. Comfortably full and fuzzy headed, Stella was relaxed enough to ask the question.

"Spare what?" Linus asked.

"Collier. You said your older brother ran the company."

"Oh, that. For a moment, I thought you were referring to royal lineage. I never gave it much thought one way or the other."

"You didn't?"

"No need," he said with a shrug. "It was always

assumed Thomas would take over. My grandfather all but named him heir apparent when we were children."

"Because he was the oldest," Stella commented.

"Probably, and he was the only one who paid attention when we visited the company museum."

"You have a company museum?"

"Doesn't every family?"

Stella shook her head. "Mine doesn't."

She leaned forward and reached for the wine bottle. Sometime during the evening, she'd taken off her running shoes and curled her legs beneath her. Toffee was long gone, having moved to her favorite chair, allowing the space between Stella and Linus to shrink.

"Damn," she declared, holding the bottle upside down. Her glass was close to empty, too. First time all night. "Should we open another bottle?"

"In my experience," Linus replied, "whenever you ask yourself if you should have another drink, the answer is always no."

"Good answer." She would have said yes and regretted it in the morning. Especially since she suspected she'd drunk most of this bottle. She definitely filled her glass more often than Linus had.

"What's it like, your company museum?"

"Your typical celebration of a four-hundred-year-old company. Yes, really," he added when she gasped. "Sounds old to Americans, but it's barely a blip in British history. Like your revolution."

He grinned. She smacked his shoulder.

"There's one section where children can mix different scents to see how they blend. I spent most of my time there while my grandfather dragged Thomas around and lectured him on duty and legacy. Susan usually spent the visits asking if we could go for ice cream."

Silently, Stella agreed with Susan's thinking. Leaning her head back, she studied Linus's chiseled features, trying to imagine him as a little boy. "Did it ever bother you? That Thomas got all your grandfather's attention?"

"What makes you think he did? Oh, because he was Grandfather's choice to carry on?" He shook his head. "If anything, I was grateful. My brother carried a lot of weight on his shoulders, and it nearly ruined his life, while I was free to pursue my own interests. Besides, Grandfather wasn't stupid. It was obvious we were on different paths."

His smile grew nostalgic. "If the museum didn't convince him, my propensity for kitchen experiments did. By the way, never light flour on fire."

"Why not?"

"Trust me—just don't."

He punctuated his advice with a stretch, his arm reaching across the back of the sofa. Stella pulled her legs tighter, saving the feeling of security currently enveloping them. "Sounds like you were a natural-born chemist."

"And Thomas was a natural-born CEO, bossy git that he is. Made the division of labor quite easy."

"What about your sister?"

"Susan? Took her a little longer to find her place, but that had nothing to do with Thomas being in charge. All and all, I'd say we all mesh rather nicely."

"You're lucky." A smart person would come back with a clever answer like how a lot of family businesses had conflicts or some other response that deflected the conversation back to Linus. The smart answer, however, didn't want to come off her tongue. "You knew what you wanted to do."

"Are you saying a life of corporate finance wasn't your life's calling? No stories about little ten-year-old Stella Russo sitting in the kitchen playing with the calculator?"

She rolled her eyes. "Hardly." Ten-year-old Stella Russo was reading juvenile historical fiction and being told to stop daydreaming. "I didn't choose my career path until I was in college."

"What made you decide on finance?" He shifted his position so he was looking at her straight on, the genuine interest in his eyes catching her by surprise. Between the wine and his sincerity, she found herself answering honestly. "Because it wasn't law or medicine."

She'd never said the words out loud before. Having done so, she rushed to explain. "My sister is a neurosurgeon, and my brother is a criminal defense attorney."

"So rather than copy one of them, you chose a path to call your own."

"Something like that." More like she took a path unlikely to invite comparison.

"Your parents must be very proud."

"Of Camilla and Joe? Very."

"I meant of all three of you."

She shrugged and looked down at her glass. Only a few swallows of golden liquid remained. She was more relaxed than she had been in years. Whether it was from too much wine or the security of Linus's company, she couldn't be sure, but thoughts she usually kept buried were suddenly comfortable bubbling to the surface. "I think I'm like your sister, still finding my way."

"No crime in that," Linus said.

"You're not a Russo," she replied. "My father has very high expectations." She tipped back the rest of her glass before continuing. "My grandfather died when my father was in high school. He had to quit school and take over Grandpa's fruit and vegetable market to support the family. Turned it in to a regional corporation. Biggest distributor in New England."

"Quite an accomplishment."

"It is." But it wasn't enough for Kevin Russo. "My dad hates that he didn't go to college. Didn't even graduate high school. Meanwhile, my uncle went to Yale and so did all his kids. Uncle Donny's always bragging about them. So, Dad has made it his mission to make sure we are bragworthy, too. Camilla and Joe are fulfilling the mission admirably."

"You don't include yourself in the list?"

"Oh, sure. I'm doing peachy." Reaching for the bottle, she turned it upside down again and watched as a trickle dripped into her glass. Barely enough to count as a swallow but better than nothing. She drained her glass.

"Did you know I finished in the top five percent of my glass at graduate school?" she asked.

"Congratulations."

"Thank you. Camilla and Joe finished first."

"I'm pretty sure a potential employer would call that splitting hairs."

Says the man who worked for his family. "I got hired by the top consulting firm in Manhattan."

"See?"

"Yep. Lasted a whole five months before I blew it."

The room wobbled when she set her glass down. She sat up and pressed her hands to her knees to still the movement, shivering slightly as her body mourned losing Linus's body heat. This wasn't the kind of confession that deserved coziness.

"I'd been doing great," she told him. "Working a ton—seventy, seventy-five hours a week—but that wasn't new. I've always had to work more than others to keep ahead. Plus, I was working on this project that had huge potential. The kind of project that can turn an employee into a rock star."

She remembered how the night before, she and her father had talked about the project's make-or-break potential.

You need to make them notice you, her father had said.

"Then one morning I was on my way to work, and I froze. Right in the middle of Fifty-Second Street. Couldn't move forward or backward."

As she expected, when she looked over her shoulder, Linus wore a frown. "Eventually, I managed to cross the street, but that's as far as I got. Standing on the sidewalk, shaking. I couldn't talk. I could barely breathe."

The moment was etched in her memory forever. The way the building seemed to stretch and grow larger. The rush of white noise in her ears.

And the fear. The paralyzing fear that if she went inside, it would kill her.

"A coworker took me to the emergency room. Severe burnout is what the doctor said. I just knew that I couldn't go back to work. I wanted to, but I didn't want to. If that makes sense."

"What did you do then?"

"What could I do?" she replied. "Went home and told my parents I'd messed up."

"I wouldn't say you—"

Stella was on too much of a confession roll to hear him. "Do you have any idea how humiliating that was? There were Camilla and Joe racking up the accolades, and here I was, pulling up the rear. Again. So, I ran away. Couldn't face the idea of running into someone I knew and having to explain. Figured England was far enough to get my act together."

She flung herself back against the sofa, back to the security of Linus's proximity. "Now you know why I need to do the best job possible while I'm here. I need to show them that what happened in New York was an anomaly. To prove I'm not a disappointment." Her voice cracked on the last part. Damn alcohol.

A reassuring hand cupped her shoulder. Stella found herself pulled toward Linus in a semihug. She rested her head on his shoulder and drank in the comfort. "I don't think you're a disappointment," he said.

"No offense, but how would you know?"

"Your story. You may have crashed, but you picked yourself up and came to England. If you ask me, that shows resilience. Disappointments aren't resilient."

Stella pulled back far enough to look into his face. What she saw was a friendly smile. No mocking or sign of insincerity. "That might be the nicest thing anyone has ever said to me," she said.

"Then you're clearly not receiving enough compliments."

Stella met his smile.

Suddenly, the room grew small. Reduced to the sofa and the air around them. A lazy heat started low in Stella's belly, a longing for closeness. She wanted to feel a man's hands on her skin. To feel desirable. She looked into Linus's eyes and saw a beautiful gray sky. Scrambling to her knees, she let herself fall into them. Deeper. Closer. Until her lips met his…

CHAPTER FOUR

"STELLA..." HE BREATHED her name into her mouth like it was a prayer. She felt his fingers sliding along her cheeks until they cradled her face. He combed back her hair and pulled away.

"Stella," he repeated. "You've had too much to drink."

He was rejecting her.

"Well, isn't this humiliating," she said, backing away. "I..."

Linus backed away, too. The tenderness she imagined in his gaze had morphed into embarrassment. "I should go," he said.

"Yeah, I think that's a good idea."

She kept her attention glued to the coffee table while Linus got up and limped toward the front door. "I'm sorry," he said when he reached the landing. "But I don't think either of us wants to do something we'll regret."

Not trusting herself to speak, Stella only thanked God for that. She'd rambled on about her failings and made a fool out of herself, but at least she hadn't done something she'd regret.

*** *** ***

Linus closed his front door and collapsed against it. That might have been one of most difficult things he had ever done. *Give yourself a pat on the back, old boy. You behaved like a gentleman.* Eighteen months ago, if a beautiful woman threw herself in his arms, he would have kissed the daylights out of her. Lips that soft and delicious? How could he resist?

But he did resist. Had to. It was clear his neighbor needed a friend far more than she needed sex.

I need to prove I'm not a disappointment.

How could the woman with whom he'd spent the evening disappoint anyone? It was inconceivable. She was funny. Beautiful. Smart.

His rejection probably hadn't helped her self-esteem issues. Still, he'd done the right thing. Maybe that meant he was evolving into a better person. Because for once he cared more about helping a woman than seducing her.

Now if he could only stop thinking about how amazing Stella's lips tasted, he'd be fine.

When she woke up, Stella decided the best recourse was to pretend the night before never happened. Easier said than done, since she woke with a pounding headache, but she pretended that was the result of stress.

"A believable excuse, right?" she asked Toffee.

The cat had spent the night at the foot of Stella's bed, her imported silk cat bed apparently not comfortable enough.

Toffee yawned and rolled on her side.

Didn't matter what the cat thought. Burying the humiliating experience was far preferable to recalling what an ass she'd made of herself. Between telling Linus about New York and kissing him...

Yeah, pretending it never happened was definitely the best idea.

Instead, she spent the morning taking inventory. One of her assigned tasks was to catalog Dame Agnes's personal belongings. After six decades of performing, the woman had amassed large collections of memorabilia, objets d'art, jewelry and other items. According to Peter, some pieces were bequeathed to friends and colleagues, but the majority were to be inventoried and then either sold or donated as part of a historical collection. Stella's job was to track down as many of the known items as possible, especially the theater souvenirs, many of which were quite rare and valuable. The task was surprisingly interesting, and burying herself in a spreadsheet was exactly what she needed. If she were focused on hunting objects, she wouldn't have time to think about the feel of Linus's hands on her skin. Or how comfortable and at ease he'd made her feel.

"Have you seen a gold-and-enamel cigarette holder, Mrs. Churchill?" she asked later that morning.

The housekeeper looked up from the desk she was polishing. "A gold-and-enamel what?"

"Cigarette holder. It says on this spreadsheet that Dame Agnes had one from the show *Suite Envy*, but it doesn't seem to be in the media room with the rest of the items."

"And you think I know where it is?"

"I was hoping," Stella replied.

The older woman swatted the desk with her dust cloth. "It could be anywhere. Mrs. Moreland was always taking those things out to show people. Once I found a crown in the bathroom."

Great. Another item unaccounted for. Circling the item on the spreadsheet, Stella made a mental note to ask Peter when the list was last updated. So far three of the first six items were a bust.

"Thanks anyway," she said to Mrs. Churchill. "Oh, and thank you for watching Toffee while I went for my run yesterday. Sorry I was late getting back."

"That reminds me," Mrs. Churchill replied. "Did you take one of the wine bottles from the rack? Not that it's any of my business, but I noticed you were one short."

There went her plan to erase last night. "Mr. Collier came over after our run for dinner and he opened the bottle," Stella said as she pretended to study the spreadsheet. The eleven-by-seventeen paper made a perfect screen to hide her warm cheeks. "He said he'd buy a replacement bottle."

Meaning she would see him again. If anything could be worse than last night's rejection, it would be seeing pity in Linus's eyes.

The sad thing was that she didn't know what she'd been thinking. She had zero interest in a relationship, casual or otherwise. But then she'd lost herself in those blue-gray eyes, and kissing him felt…natural.

Was there some kind of self-help group for people who self-sabotaged? Screwing up was a common thread lately. Mess up her job. Nearly mess up another job. Get drunk and kiss the only friend she had in London.

You'd think she didn't want to be successful.

Oblivious to her mental turmoil, Mrs. Churchill shrugged. "Don't matter to me either way. Most likely he bought the bottle in the first place. He was always bringing one when Mrs. Moreland invited him for dinner."

Stella recalled how capable Linus had looked opening the wine. The conversation had opened a floodgate of images that made her stomach turn over. She kept her gaze on the spreadsheet. "So he said."

Mrs. Churchill continued. "Mrs. Moreland

loved to have him over, that's for sure. Said he prettied up the place. Can't disagree. Man wears a suit well. Her highness liked him, too." She nodded at Toffee, who was on her perch looking out the terrace door.

"He's a hard man not to like," Stella replied. Suddenly she needed some air. Excusing herself, she stepped onto the terrace, taking a moment to scratch Toffee's chin on the way by. "I'll be right back, Toff. Then I'll give you your daily brushing."

Whereas yesterday's weather had been perfect, today's was merely nice. A collection of cumulus clouds made the sunshine inconsistent. A good thing, actually, since the air was humid. Wishing it was long enough to pull into a ponytail, Stella brushed the hair from her face.

There was music coming from next door. At first, she tried to ignore the noise, but then a woman's laugh rang out.

Stella's stomach sank. Social sabbatical, her ass. He could have simply told her he wasn't interested. To further rub salt in her wound, they sounded like they were seated by his bedroom. What had he done? Left her and immediately called someone else?

Intending to move inside, where she could ignore the distraction, Stella stepped toward the terrace door. That's when the woman laughed again.

What was she like? The woman Linus preferred. He probably liked them blonde and
sophisticated. Or did he prefer brunette and sophisticated? Assuming he preferred this woman
at all. She could be a business associate.

Because women giggled uproariously all the
time during business meetings.

She needed to check this woman out. Not because she was jealous, but to satisfy her curiosity. If she stood in the corner of the terrace, near
Linus's clump of trees, she could peer through
the branches without being seen.

You're going to regret this, the voice in her
head said. *He's going to be in the paisley robe
looking sexy as ever and you're going to regret
spying. Just go inside.*

She looked through the branches.

No robe, thank goodness. Linus had his back
to her, but she could see he wore a pale blue shirt,
the cotton stretched across his broad shoulders a
taunting reminder of what it felt like be nestled
beside him. The woman, meanwhile, wasn't at all
what Stella expected. She was short, with large
breasts and a thick waist, and she wore a giant,
soppy smile.

This was a foolish idea. Stella started to back
away.

"Oh, hello!"

Damn.

At the woman's greeting, Linus swiveled in his seat. Stella stepped out of the shadows. "Hello," she greeted.

"Can we help you with something?" the woman asked.

"I… I didn't realize you had company," Stella replied. "I had a question for Linus, but it can wait. Sorry to interrupt."

"Nonsense, you're not interrupting anything. Is she, Linus?"

"Um, no. Not at all." Stella couldn't decide if the awkwardness in his reply was real or her imagination. Same went for the color in his cheeks. "What was it you wanted to ask?"

Good question. What did she want to ask? "The wine. Do you remember the brand? Mrs. Churchill said she'd buy a replacement bottle."

"Mrs. Churchill doesn't have to go out of her way. I told you I would replace it."

"She doesn't mind. It's on her way home. And this way you won't have to make a special trip over here."

"I don't mind." He stood up to face her. That's when Stella saw the reason for the woman's soppy smile. A baby sat cradled in the crook of Linus's arm.

"Oh," he replied, noting her open mouth, "this is my nephew. I'm babysitting while his parents attend parents' day at my niece's summer camp."

"He's adorable," Stella replied. Even from a distance she could see the baby's plump cheeks.

"He is a handsome fellow, isn't he? Takes after his uncle, don't you, Noel?"

Still in her chair, the woman cleared her throat. "As usual, it looks like I'm going to have to introduce myself. I'm Susan Collier."

The baby sister Linus mentioned. She was jealous of Linus's sister. *Curious*, she corrected. And she was relieved because she hadn't interrupted a date. "Stella Russo," she replied.

"The pet sitter."

"Estate manager," Linus corrected. "She's also helping to catalog Dame Agnes's property."

"Sounds interesting."

"It is," Stella replied. Susan Collier had a very sharp stare to go with her sharp tongue that made Stella wonder if the pet-sitter comment had been meant as an insult or a test.

"Ignore her," Linus said. "She came out of the womb sarcastic."

"Only way I could survive in this family. It's a pleasure to meet you, Stella. Would you care to join us?"

"Thank you, but I have to get to back to work. I really only wanted to check on Linus's ankle."

"Ankle? I thought you wanted to ask about wine," Susan said.

"Yes. That, too. Wine and his ankle. How is it, Linus?"

"Better. I taped it this morning for stability. With any luck, I'll be running in a few weeks."

"I hope so. I'd feel terrible if being my running guide caused you problems."

"No problems. It was my own stupidity."

They could have been apologizing for the kiss. In fact, part of Stella wondered if, behind the words, they were. Certainly felt awkward enough.

The rustling of leaves filled the silence between them. Stella was about to end the moment with a goodbye, but Noel beat her to the punch. He squirmed and made tiny noises of discomfort.

"I think someone is getting hungry. Rosalind packed a bottle of mother's milk. Hand him over, Linus, and I'll feed him. You two can…" She gestured between them. "Talk."

Easier said than done. The words Stella needed wouldn't form. They sat there in a giant tangle, clogging her throat.

"Look, about last night," Linus started. "If I gave you the wrong impression…"

"It was the wine," she immediately shot back. "I had way too much and acted stupidly. I didn't mean to put you in such an awkward position."

"It's not that I don't find you attractive…" She held up a hand. No need for false compliments.

"You made it clear you're not looking for anything beyond friendship right now, and truthfully neither am I. In fact, until I get my career back on track, relationships are totally on the back burner. And a one-night stand would have made things super awkward, so I appreciate you being a gentleman."

"*Gentleman* is a bit generous." He smiled as he said it, but she spied a cloud crossing his features. It wasn't the first time he'd drawn back when she complimented his kindness. Why?

"I hope what happened won't ruin our friendship," she told him.

"I'm all right if you are," he replied.

"Right as rain." She was relieved. That's why her insides felt buoyant. She could use a friend, and she enjoyed Linus's company. He was the first person she'd met in a long time who made her feel comfortable.

Or do you mean special?

No, she meant comfortable. Special was what she'd felt when she had looked in his eyes last night. And she was not going to repeat that mistake. She would just have to tuck *special* as far back in her brain as possible.

"So that's the pet sitter," Susan said, once Stella disappeared behind her wall. "She's pretty."

Linus hadn't moved since Stella said goodbye.

"Estate manager, and yes, she is pretty. But no, I'm not interested in her."

"Did I say anything?"

His sister didn't have to. After twenty-eight years together, Linus knew her thoughts. "We're friends, nothing more."

"If you say so." She sat down, baby Noel draped over her shoulder.

"I know that voice," Linus replied.

"What are you talking about?"

"You're using your 'I don't believe you' voice. You're playing armchair psychiatrist, looking for things that aren't there. I'm not romantically interested in Stella. We're friends and that's all."

"Fine. I'm not trying to read into anything. You're allowed to have female friends."

"Thank you."

"However, if I were to offer an opinion…"

Here we go. "Go ahead." He sat down. Susan's opinions could get long-winded. "What's your opinion?" As if he didn't know what she was about to say.

"You can't spend the rest of your life feeling guilty. What happened with Victoria wasn't your fault."

"I didn't help matters." A more sensitive man, a more empathetic man, would have recognized Victoria's troubles. But no, he'd been focused on conquest, and once he succeeded, he'd moved on. "I should have realized how unhappy she was."

"How? No one realized, Linus. Not even her family."

So everyone continued to tell him, but he had been Victoria's lover. The role demanded an intimacy that he'd failed to achieve.

What Susan and the rest of the world failed to realize was that his guilt ran far deeper than Victoria. For years, he'd treated women as objects to pursue, writing off their post-breakup insults as brokenhearted rants. They were the problem, he told himself. After all, he never pretended the relationships were anything but physical and casual.

Ultimately, it didn't matter if he was the direct or an indirect factor in her death. He was still a bloody ass.

"One would think you'd be happy for me," he said to her. "I'm in a platonic relationship with a woman."

"Break out the champagne. Hell hath frozen over."

"Damn straight." He needed this friendship with Stella, if not to help her, then to help himself. To teach himself how to be a decent human being.

"And, before you ask, the lady is not interested, either," he added. At least, not when sober. "She's one hundred percent about the job. Makes Thomas look rational."

Susan let out a whistle. Their brother tended to commit in the extreme, including managing the company. "Sounds hard-core for a pet sitter."

She wasn't a pet sitter, but Linus didn't feel like arguing the point. Besides, after their conversation last night, he wondered if Stella's drive to succeed wasn't powered by something deeper. All her talk about coming up short in comparison to her siblings. "Her family is very accomplished," he said. "Her parents, her siblings all have successful careers. Lawyers, surgeons."

"And she feels like the family outlier. I understand."

Yes, she did, better than most. "But you carved your own space."

"Wasn't easy, what with Mother always criticizing and living with you two Greek gods." Linus laughed at her description. "Honestly, it wasn't until I found Lewis and realized I was lovable on my own merits that I finally grew comfortable in my own skin."

Another reason why he placed such value in maintaining a platonic relationship with Stella. She needed someone to prove she mattered regardless of what she did for a living, and that could only happen if she trusted him. For once, the woman's needs mattered more than his.

Maybe he was evolving.

He and his sister spent the afternoon cooing over Noel's cuteness until the baby fell asleep. "I'm not sure who is more tired," he told Thomas. "Smiling at a baby all day is a lot of work."

His brother just laughed and picked up the collection of toys and snacks left strewn around Linus's living room. "He is deceptively charming, isn't he? Must be the Collier in him."

"Which version? You, me or Dad?"

"Right now, I'd say he's leaning toward you. The other day, we were out for tea and some random woman gave him a treat simply because he smiled at her."

"Better watch it," Linus said, "or he'll be trying to steal kisses on the schoolyard before you realize it."

"Well, at this rate he won't have to try too hard, will he? Another one of his uncle's qualities it looks like he inherited."

Hopefully not, thought Linus.

"Noticed you're limping. Don't tell me, you tripped over my boy?"

"Nah. Rolled it while out for a run." Briefly, while Thomas buckled Noel into his carrier, Linus relayed what happened with Toffee and how that had led to him going for a run with his new neighbor.

"Can't say I blame her," Thomas said, regarding Stella's stress about her meeting with Teddy. "Although next time you want to calm someone down, I'd take it easier. You're lucky you didn't break your bloody leg. You must really like this woman."

"We're friends. Nothing more," Linus replied. "Neither of us is interested in anything more."

"Well, friends are nice, too." Thomas looked like he was about to say something more, but thankfully he changed his mind. Linus was not in the mood to have a second conversation about his friendship with Stella. Honestly, was it so difficult to believe he had a platonic relationship with her? How much of a playboy had he been for both his siblings to jump straight to the same conclusion?

A few moments passed in silence, Thomas chewing his lip as he finished his last-minute gathering. "You know you can talk to me if you need to," he said once his arms were full. "About anything. Lord knows you were there for me when Rosalind and I had our problems."

"Because you and Rosalind were meant to be together. Anyone with two heads could see how much you loved one another. Trust me, this isn't the same thing. Not by a long shot."

Thomas wasn't like their sister, thank goodness, and didn't press. Inside, Linus let out a grateful sigh of relief. He wasn't in the mood to explain things again.

Seriously, how many times could he explain that he was not romantically interested in Stella?

Even if he had dreamed of her kiss all evening long.

Having declined Thomas's invitation for dinner, Linus poured himself a glass of stout and limped back to the garden. Not that he didn't love his family, but he wasn't in the mood to play fifth wheel.

The air had grown thicker over the past few hours. Looking up, he saw the beginnings of dark clouds. Rain was coming. Usually, he liked the fresh, musky smell that permeated the air just before a storm. It was the smell of anticipation.

Tonight, the scent left him with a hollow feeling. If he didn't know better, he'd say it felt like loneliness. Felt lonely.

More likely, he was simply unsettled after all the talk about Victoria. And Stella.

He wondered what his neighbor was up to. Was she, like him, planning on a night of paperwork and television?

There was only one way to tell. Setting down his drink, he limped over to his favorite rock. Stella's garden was empty. The terrace doors and windows were locked tight. Crickets chirped in the emptiness. How they made it to the top of his building, he hadn't a clue, but their noise could be heard along with the steady hum of an air-conditioning unit. He imagined Stella sitting at her dining room table, carefully balancing a plate of whatever Mrs. Churchill made so she didn't spill on the paperwork spread before her. Occasionally talking to Toffee who, no doubt, wanted whatever was on the plate.

Last night's conversation bothered him in ways he couldn't describe. The way she talked about not measuring up, as though life were a competition for a prize. She was a beautiful, intelligent woman. How was it that he could see her laudability within five minutes of meeting her, yet she couldn't?

Why did it matter to him?

Because you like her.

Of course he did. They were friends, and friends cared about one another. Granted, his feelings were a bit intense for someone he'd just met, but he blamed the intensity on his issues. Bottom line was that two years from now, he didn't want to hear that sweet, tightly wound Stella had had another breakdown. Or worse. The girl needed to know her worth, and he, as a friend, needed to help her unwind and believe in herself.

An idea started to form.

CHAPTER FIVE

STELLA WAS FLUMMOXED. She'd spent the last week gathering and organizing the items on Dame Agnes's inventory list, and, by her count, at least a dozen items were missing. Things like a silver cigarette lighter. A pair of garnet earrings. A topaz brooch. All small to midsize, and all things that Dame Agnes could have given away. Or that could have been removed from the house unnoticed.

For fun, she searched the online auction houses for Agnes Moreland memorabilia, but the only items were Playbills and autographed photos.

"I don't suppose you know," she asked Toffee.

If she did, the cat wasn't talking.

Tired of staring at pages with no answers, Stella tossed her pen on the table. "How about I get my apron and give you a brushing, Toff?"

Brushing Toffee's white coat was one of her daily duties. The first time, Stella found her skirt covered with white fur. Since then, she'd made a point of wearing a protective apron.

As soon as she saw the brush, Toffee jumped on the sofa and flopped on her side. "You are so spoiled. In my next life, I'm coming back as a cat so someone will stroke my fur every afternoon."

Not that she'd tell Toffee, but the ritual was one of her favorite parts of the day. The slow, methodical strokes were like meditation. Her shoulder muscles would relax and she'd finish in a calmer mood. Maybe, when she went home, she'd get a cat, too. So engrossed was she in her task that when the doorbell rang, she didn't hear it. Only when she heard Mrs. Churchill talking to someone did she realize there was a visitor.

Please don't let it be Teddy Moreland.

It was Linus. "Hello, stranger," he greeted. A grin broke across her face. He was dressed for work, in a gray suit similar to the one he'd worn when they first met, only instead of the glasses in his breast pocket, they were perched on the bridge of his nose. He gave off a very sexy professor vibe as a result.

"Hello to you, too. I haven't seen you all week." She'd kept an ear out for noise every time she stepped outside, but his backyard had been quiet, and his house was dark whenever she looked over from her balcony.

"Sorry for that. Been burning the midnight oil for a bit. Joint meeting with sales and marketing. How goes the battle?"

"If you mean the daily quest to make Toffee's life as easy as possible? Look for yourself." She leaned against the back of the sofa so he could see the cat sprawled across her lap.

"Looks to be going well. I'm sure she has complaints, though."

"She's a cat. Of course, she has complaints. I see you're still limping."

"Only at the end of the day," he said as he took a seat across from her. Across from, not next to.

"I guess that means you're not here to see about a run."

"No. Actually I'm here for another reason. Would you stay, Mrs. Churchill? It involves you as well."

"Me?" The woman's confused face matched Stella's. "What do you need me for?"

"I need a favor," Linus replied. He looked back at Stella. "Have you seen any of London since you've arrived?"

"Sure, I have." The other morning she'd run a few errands and seen Piccadilly Circus.

"I mean, really seen it? Buckingham Palace, Trafalgar Square, the Eye... You do know what the London Eye is?"

"Don't be ridiculous. Everyone's heard of the Eye." It was the big Ferris wheel thing on the other side of the Thames. "But I'm not here on vacation. Sightseeing isn't part of the agenda."

"It is tonight," he announced. "I refuse to let

you spend a year in London without seeing everything our city has to offer."

He wanted to take her sightseeing? Memories of what happened the last time they went out together flashed before her eyes. "I don't think... I have a lot of work to do."

"All work and no play makes Stella a very dull girl."

"Are you calling me dull?" The words came out louder than expected, startling Toffee off her lap. "I have a job to do. I'm still trying to sort out the inventory inaccuracies."

"Which will still be there in the morning."

"And what about Toffee?" She'd already explained why she didn't treat the animal like a regular pet.

"I don't think Toffee would like sightseeing." He responded to her glare with a smirk. "Toffee is precisely why I asked Mrs. Churchill to stay. Would you be willing to watch the cat for a few hours while I show Stella Tower Bridge?"

Dear Lord, not only was he asking Mrs. Churchill to stay and cat sit, but he was making puppy-dog eyes. "Mrs. Churchill shouldn't be expected to—"

The housekeeper cut her off. "You know I could never say no to you."

Who could? Those eyes were impossible to resist, all big and steel blue.

"I'd be glad to stay a few hours," Mrs. Churchill continued. "It'll do you some good to get out of the house, Ms. Russo."

With a sigh, Stella looked at the dining room table and the spreadsheets strewn across the surface. If she were serious about doing the job right, she'd stay home and begin grouping items into lots. That's what Camilla or Joseph would do. They'd buckle down and focus on the task at hand.

She turned back to Linus. There was something anxious beneath his plaintive expression, as though he needed her to say yes. Her imagination, she decided, although her stomach fluttered anyway.

This was her first time in London. And honestly, she doubted even her driven siblings would be able to resist Linus Collier's plaintive expression.

"All right," she said. "Let me get my walking shoes."

"It's at least two hundred years old. There's a note in the paperwork saying the count sent it to her with a marriage proposal after watching her onstage. I mean, who does that?"

"Very rich men with very little common sense," Linus replied.

They were on their way to dinner on the South

Bank of the Thames. Linus had promised her a dinner with a view that he said would take her breath away.

On the way, Linus asked about her day, which he probably regretted, because she'd been chatting his ear off ever since. She couldn't help it. Dame Agnes Moreland had been an amazing woman. Every item she inventoried had a spectacular origin story. More than once, Stella had stopped what she was doing to investigate a source online. That's how she learned the backstory behind the bracelet Count Domenici gave Agnes.

"What's more," she continued, "she kept these things in her jewelry box like they were something she bought at a local jeweler. Clearly the woman didn't worry about theft."

"You mean the woman whose cat is wearing a diamond collar? Definitely not."

She matched his grin. "I know Peter was talking about selling the pieces, but I'm hoping he'll reconsider."

"In favor of what?"

"A collection of some sort, maybe?" She didn't know. "I just think it would be a shame to sell them off at auction when people might enjoy learning about Dame Agnes's life. You know she left diaries, too?" Stella had lost another few hours to reading them in the name of research. "What?"

Linus was studying her with an odd expression. She couldn't tell if it was amusement or appreciation. There was definitely a sparkle in his eyes. "Your expression," he said. "It's obvious how much you're enjoying yourself."

"I've always been fascinated by artifacts and antiques," she said. "There's something almost magical about holding a piece of someone's history in the palm of your hand."

"I'm surprised you didn't go into the field, then."

"Business was more practical." And a fascination didn't make a career. At least not one of note. *The world is full of baristas who majored in history,* her father liked to say. "Anyway, I sent a long email to Peter this morning with my suggestion and letting him know I've made notes on the pieces. Hopefully, he'll consider it. If not, the expanded backstories might drive up prices."

"If you believe that strongly, why not offer to stay and curate the collection yourself?"

She liked how he thought she was capable enough to do the job. "First of all, I'm not an experienced curator, and besides, I already have a plan, remember? I'm heading back to New York." Didn't matter how much she enjoyed her current task. She had things to prove.

The London Eye came into view. The giant

wheel, with its oval passenger pods was already lit for evening. A pale pink circle in the blue sky.

"Best way to see as much of London as possible in one shot," Linus said.

Stella looked up at the top car, hovering over four hundred feet above the city. Small wonder there was a long line waiting to board. Her stomach rumbled in protest at having to wait.

"I know you suggested dinner and a ride, but do you suppose we could do dinner first?" she asked. "I'm starving."

A sparkle appeared in his twilight-colored eyes. "Or we could dine and ride. The two aren't mutually exclusive."

"Fine with me." A hot dog and a soft drink while standing in line worked for her.

To her surprise, however, Linus took her elbow and, bypassing the crowd, walked straight to the entrance.

"Right on time, Mr. Collier," the woman at the ticket wicket replied when he introduced himself. "Your car will be arriving any moment."

Stella looked at him through her fallen bangs. "You reserved a car?"

"I did more than that," he replied.

Since the wheel moved slowly, there was no need to wait until it stopped moving to board. Passengers could walk on and off the cars with ease. As they strolled down the ramp, Stella noticed the car approaching contained a table set for two. It had a white tablecloth and a pair of artificial candles—real ones being too much of a fire hazard. There were two plates, two large goblets and an ice bucket positioned on the floor nearby.

Stella's insides swooped. "A private dinner?" For her?

"Knowing how you hate leaving Toffee with a sitter, I was afraid you might grow impatient taking time for both dinner and sightseeing. Therefore, I decided to multitask. Of course, if you're feeling awkward, we can tell them to let on a few more passengers."

A worker hurried past them to place a large square box in the center before hurrying off again. Pizza. That's when she noticed the ice bucket didn't contain champagne, but rather a growler of British brown ale. "I'm not sure we have enough food for guests," she said. The pizza only had eight slices.

"I was trying to stay low-key. The gesture felt romantic enough as it was."

And heaven forbid she get the wrong idea. "Pizza and beer are perfect," she replied.

The pod doors slid closed, leaving them to begin their ascent. The Plexiglas space was purposely designed to hold multiple passengers. Despite this, it felt very small and crowded. Linus was the kind of man whose presence took up a lot of space, no matter what size the room. She could feel his energy all around them.

While he busied himself with pouring the beer, Stella took a slice of pizza and walked to the window. Linus was right. London was a beautiful city. Although sunset was still a few hours away, Big Ben blocked the late-day glare, allowing them a perfect view of Westminster Abbey and Westminster Bridge. Across the way tour boats drifted up and down the river. They ate standing up, and as they moved higher, she spotted Tower Bridge in the distance. She could also see Trafalgar Square with its columned tribute to Admiral Nelson in the center.

"It's amazing," she told Linus.

He took a sip from his beer. "The best time for a ride is right at sunset, but this isn't bad. Look off in the distance. You should be able to just see Buckingham Palace through the trees."

For the next several minutes, Linus played tour guide, pointing out landmarks and providing amusing anecdotes. Buildings he didn't know, he cheekily made up. Stella guessed this when he described one building as the Ministry of Monkey Business.

"You've done this before, haven't you?" she remarked. His patter was too smooth and polished to be the first time.

He ducked his head, pink streaking his cheekbones. "Once or twice. Never served them pizza and beer, though."

More like champagne and truffles, she bet. Knowing he put in the extra effort to do something different made her feel special. Respected.

"Which building is your company?" she asked.

"Hold on." Setting his beer on the window ledge, he stepped behind her and grasped her shoulders, gently angling her body eastward. "Do you see that high-rise tower with the gray slanted roof? Next to what looks like a greenway? Colliers is about two blocks northeast."

"I'll take your word for it." All Stella could see were rooftops. Linus remained behind her with his hands resting on her shoulders. The half embrace was warm and soothing, like being draped in a blanket. He'd long since shed his jacket in favor of rolled shirtsleeves. Stella swore she could feel his shirt buttons brushing the zipper of her dress. If she relaxed her neck, her head would rest on his shoulder.

"Are you having a good time?" he asked, the timbre of his voice running through them both.

"Very." Hearing the way her voice sounded— like a breathy whisper—startled her back to reality. She pulled away, clearing an imaginary frog as she did so. "Very," she repeated. "I wish we had something like this in New York. We have the Empire State Building and the Freedom Tower, but…well, I guess they offer the same thing except you're not moving." She was babbling. Where was her beer?

"Here." Coming to her rescue, as usual, Linus appeared with her glass. "Need more?"

"Please." Her cheeks were still warm.

He lifted the growler from the bucket and filled both their glasses. "Speaking of New York. You never said what it is you did there, or rather, what it is you hope to return to."

"Didn't I?"

"Only that you worked for a consulting firm," he replied, handing over her glass.

"Not a consulting firm. The top international consulting firm in the city." Every time she said that, a bundle of nerves went off in her stomach. "It's incredibly competitive to get hired. They only take the top candidates."

"Congratulations, then."

"Thank you." But the good wishes felt undeserved. Was that why she was doing such a hard sales job?

"They must think very highly of you if they were willing to grant you a leave of absence."

"Either that or they're afraid of a lawsuit." It was a joke, but it fell awkwardly. Maybe because it wasn't out of the realm of possibility. "Anyway, I was hired to do risk assessment. Analyze companies' plans for expansion and so on."

"Sounds interesting."

She hoped so. "It's definitely a field with room for growth, that's for sure." Sipping her drink, she strolled to the other side of the pod, where St. Paul's dome could be seen shining in the sunlight.

"Which is important," Linus remarked. "Growth potential."

"Of course. Not much of a career if you can't move up the ladder."

"Number one or nothing."

"What?" He'd spoken softly, almost as if talking to himself.

"I said, number one or nothing. You gave me the impression that it's your family motto."

Right. She remembered her embarrassing behavior that night. "In case you forgot, I was a little drunk. I said and did a lot of stupid things."

"No, you didn't." Said in a gentle voice, the words took Stella aback. Linus closed the distance between them. "Haven't you ever heard the phrase *in vino veritas*?"

In wine, truth. She rolled her eyes. "Wine also brings on pity parties."

"Is that what happened?"

Which time? When she bemoaned being the family loser or when she kissed him? The kiss was…a moment of weakness. A foolish overreaction to someone making her feel special.

"I have a lot of regret over what happened in

New York. I spent my entire life working my tail off only to blow it by freezing up while on the job. If you were in my shoes, wouldn't you indulge in a pity party or two?"

"I suppose I would."

But... The unspoken word hung there between them. Stella resisted rubbing her shoulders. Sometimes it felt as though Linus didn't believe her answers. He had this way of looking at her as though he were looking beyond her surface and trying to read her thoughts.

She studied him back, taking in the way he leaned against the window rail and drank his beer. The relaxed posture was deceptive. She could tell from the way his index finger tapped the railing that he was mulling over his next comment.

"Go ahead," she said. "You obviously have something you want to add."

"Not really. I was thinking, is all."

"About what?"

His attention dropped to his glass. "I couldn't help but notice that when you were talking about cataloging Agnes's memorabilia, you were so excited you were practically bouncing. Yet, when it came time to talking about the job that you call your life's goal, you had far less enthusiasm. Hardly any, to be honest."

"Because cataloging Agnes's belongings is my current job. New York is still a year away. Doesn't it make sense that I would be more enthusiastic about the work I'm actually doing? I'm sure when next spring arrives, I'll sound equally bouncy. More so."

"You're right," he said.

"I know I am." Even as she defended herself, an uneasiness twisted in her stomach. Dammit, he was making her doubt herself.

Linus again contemplating his beer didn't help. "May I ask one more question?" he asked her.

"What?" Why ask for permission? He was going to ask whether she said yes or no.

"Your plan is to climb as high up the corporate ladder as possible, right? What are you going to do if you can't move up? If you aren't able to take the risk-assessment world by storm?"

Failure wasn't an option. "This isn't like your family company where everyone stays for hundreds of years. If there isn't a promotion available at one company, I'll move to one where there is one."

"Building a career is that important?"

"Building a career that matters is that important. You wouldn't understand," she told him. "You're already successful."

"I was under the impression success was a personal definition."

"Says the man whose role in the family legacy is already secure." She slapped her drink on the table and stomped to the opposite window. The conversation left her irritated. Who was he to judge her plans?

"I'm sorry," he said from his side of the observation pod. "I didn't mean to spoil the evening. I shouldn't have said anything."

No, he shouldn't have. Why did he? "What does it matter to you what my life plans are, anyway?"

There was silence, followed by the sound of footsteps. When he spoke, his voice was close to her shoulder. "Because you're my friend," he said, "and I'm concerned about you."

"Concerned?" Stella nearly laughed, except she could tell by the tone of his voice that he was serious. A fact confirmed by the look in his eyes when she turned around. "Why?"

"You remind me of someone I used to know. Her name was Victoria. She also took things—life—very seriously. Too seriously, some might say."

"Let me guess, the two of you dated."

His expression grew somber. "We had a short relationship, yes."

"All right, I remind you of an ex-girlfriend." One, if she were to guess from his expression, that didn't leave him with fond memories. "I don't understand why that has you concerned. We aren't dating, so there's not going to be any kind of messy breakup. If anything..."

"She died."

Stella stopped talking. She hadn't stopped to think the relationship might have ended tragically.

"Apparently she had a prescription for sleeping pills."

Oh God. Stella felt sick to her stomach. She waited for Linus to say it was an accident, but there was no such reassurance. Her irritation disappeared, replaced by an ache over the regret in his voice. This was the reason for his "social sabbatical." The reason he wasn't dating.

Instinct told her there was also more to the story. Setting aside, for the time being, what he was implying about her, Stella sat down at the table. "Tell me everything," she said.

Linus ignored her invitation to sit down. He hadn't intended to talk about Victoria, hadn't planned on mentioning her at all, but listening to Stella go on about needing to prove herself triggered something. She'd looked so happy talking about curating Agnes's collection. Her face lit up. Unlike the desperation that simmered beneath the surface whenever she talked about New York. Suddenly, he'd needed to make her see the difference. Make her question if going back to New York would really make her happy.

Instead, she was asking him to confess the depths of his insensitivity. How the tables did turn.

Then again, he'd opened the door, hadn't he? Spying his half-empty glass on the table, he grabbed it and headed to the window, standing with his back to Stella and the Lambeth landscape. "She was a graphic designer. Colliers hired her when we were redesigning our packaging. She was very, very good. Took her job very seriously." Like she took everything. "The two of us hit it off."

"You had a workplace fling," Stella supplied.

"In a word? Yes. Generally I avoid them—having seen the mess my father made by marrying his secretary, I knew better. But I broke my rule with Victoria."

"She was special."

"She was a challenge." He turned so Stella could see his face, not wanting her to mistake guilt for grief. "She was adamantly opposed to an affair, but eventually I wore her down. I can be quite persuasive when I want to be."

A smile teased the ends of her mouth. "So I've noticed," she replied. "How long were you, um, together?"

"A few months. Project ended and that was it. She took the news poorly. Like I said, she took things seriously, including our relationship."

A right awful scene it had been, too. "I knew

she was tightly wound, but I should have realized there were deeper issues. If I'd paid better attention... If I were a better person..." But no. He'd behaved as he always did. "Instead, I saw she was getting ideas, and I ended things. Because I didn't do serious. Two years later..."

"Wait," Stella interrupted. "Two years? You're not blaming yourself, then, are you?"

Linus sighed. She wasn't thinking anything he hadn't thought himself. Only someone with an ego the size of Europe would think a woman was so in love with him that she'd be mourning the breakup two years later.

Thinking of the letter tucked in his nightstand drawer, he shook his head.

"Only in the sense that I was a contributing factor—one of many contributing factors, I'm sure." And it didn't negate the fact that he had behaved poorly.

"But you're talking about two years. Anything could have happened in that time. You don't know what was going on in her head."

"I got a letter."

Once again, he left Stella speechless. She sat still as a rock, with her eyes focused on her clasped hands. In a way, he was grateful she wasn't looking at him. He wasn't sure he wanted to see her expression. "I never told anyone, but it arrived the day after I heard the news. She apologized for not living up to my expectations. As if she was the problem, and not me. Victoria's sister said she'd written dozens of those letters."

"Sounds like she had a lot of demons," Stella said.

"Making my behavior all the more deplorable." Damn, but he wished people would stop letting him off the hook. "My entire life, I've been a playboy. Women were for pursuing, not for commitment. If I had taken time to see Victoria—to really see her—I would have realized she was more than tightly wound. Maybe I could have helped. Or at the very least left her alone."

After being trapped in his head for months, the words came out in a rush, eager to be free. When he finished, he felt his shoulders sag under their weight. "The whole situation made me realize I needed to rethink my behavior," he said. "How I treat women."

"So you stopped dating."

He looked down at his glass. "Better I spend the time working on myself, right?"

"Oh, Linus."

"Don't," he said. "I didn't tell you to make you feel sorry for me. It was so you'd understand why I'm worried."

Stella didn't respond. Chancing a look, Linus saw her staring at her hands, which were tightly clasped in front of her. "Do you really think me that unstable?" she asked finally.

"No. I don't think you're unstable at all. But the way you take your position, that is, the way you're so hard on yourself when you make mistakes. I don't want someone I…" The explanation stuck in his throat, forcing him to cough. "I worry. Isn't that what friends do?"

Stella continued staring at her hands. The wheel was nearing the end of its rotation. He'd paid for a second trip, but he wouldn't be surprised if Stella insisted on leaving.

"I suppose they do. I've never really had a friend close enough to pay attention before. I was always too busy working or studying or whatever."

Proving his point, Linus wanted to say, but he didn't. Instead, he gave a soft laugh. "Then it's a first for both of us."

That earned him a look. "Are you trying to tell me you don't have friends?"

"No, I've plenty. Just not women." Sisters and sisters-in-law didn't count.

"Lucky me, then."

Their car reached the landing platform. Stella glanced at the doorway, then stood up. To his surprise, however, she walked away from the door, toward him, stopping inches away. Her eyes were dark and serious as she searched his face. "I'm not Victoria," she said.

"I know." Despite their similarities, there was no confusing the two. Everything about Victoria had radiated delicacy and fragility, whereas Stella was strong and capable, more so than even she knew.

"I was burned out that day in New York. Burned out and exhausted." Reaching out to cradle his face, she forced his eyes to stay locked with hers. "And you're not a bastard. At least not to me."

"Don't get too confident. There's still time."

She didn't rise to the bait. "Don't sell yourself short."

Suddenly, her arms were wrapping around his shoulders, throwing his entire body into alert. Muscles stiffening, he tried to back away. "Stella."

"Relax," she replied. "It's only a hug. Friends can hug one another, can't they?" Without waiting for a response, she pressed herself closer, her chin coming to rest on his shoulder. "I'm honored to be your first," she whispered.

How did this happen, Linus wondered. How did his precautionary tale switch into his receiving comfort? As he slowly returned the embrace, Linus felt something shift in his chest. Something large and swooping, as though it was his insides and not the Ferris wheel resuming the ascent. It was a foreign, heady feeling that he wanted to hold on to and never let go.

What was he going to do when things began to descend?

CHAPTER SIX

Autumn

"WHAT ARE YOU doing this weekend?" Stella asked.

"Same as last weekend," Linus replied.

In other words, nothing.

The two of them were preparing for a run around St. James's Park. Since Linus's ankle had healed in mid-August, they'd made running together an afternoon habit. At first it was around the neighborhood, but as his ankle grew stronger, Linus began taking her on longer routes past historic landmarks. Sometimes they even took the Tube to run other sections of the city. It was all part of his insistence that she see more of London than one aerial tour.

Things had changed following their spin on the Eye. There was a connection between them, a closeness. Linus's confession touched her in a way she couldn't explain. The look she saw in his eyes struck her square in the chest and squeezed until she wanted nothing more than to hug away his pain. Ironic, since he began the conversation by suggesting she was the one in crisis. It wasn't until after the ride ended and they were on their way home that it occurred to her she should be angry about his presumption. But by then she couldn't work up the energy. Besides, she couldn't remember the last time someone had expressed concern about her well-being without the conversation leaving Stella feeling like she was the one messing up. Since the day they met, Linus had had her back. The least she could do was have his.

"Why are you interested in my plans for the weekend?" Linus asked.

"I, um…" His leg muscles flexed as he stretched his thigh, momentarily distracting her. He was the only person she knew who could wear neon-green Lycra and look masculine.

"I have to go to Berkshire. I need to inventory Agnes's country house."

"Looking for a cat sitter, are you? I'd be glad to keep an eye on Miss Toffee for you."

"Actually, I'm taking Toffee with me. It's her house, after all." Not to mention, she'd miss the little fur ball sleeping at the foot of her bed. Over the past few weeks, she'd come to think of Toffee more as a pet than a responsibility. She made for terrific company. The perfect distraction for when late-night dreams conflated friendly hugs with more intimate acts.

"I was wondering if you would come with me," she said.

"Away with you for the weekend?"

The way he said the words made her insides squirrelly. "You don't have to come with me. Toffee and I can rent a car. I just thought it might be nice to have the company. Especially someone who knew the area. Didn't you say you used to live near there?"

"What you're really asking is if I want to be your chauffeur for the weekend."

"Not at all. I just thought it would be nice to have company. I brought up the area thing because you're always tells me to see more of the UK, and I figured you could play tour guide."

"Relax, luv. I was teasing. I think it's a splendid idea."

"You do?" Stella didn't realize how anxious she'd been about his response until her insides relaxed.

"Absolutely. I'd love to go away with you for the weekend." He was teasing again. The smirk at the end of his sentence said so.

Now, if only her squirrelly stomach would get the message.

It was cold and raw when the three of them departed Saturday morning. A typical English fall day. Linus and Stella sat in the front of his sports car, while in the back seat, Toffee sat in her travel carrier, blinking at them with annoyance. For the first part of the ninety-minute drive, Stella entertained herself by watching the passing landscape. It was a beautiful mix of suburban and pastoral. The foliage was a mosaic of red, brown and yellow interrupted every so often by a service station or steeple. Occasionally she would see a stretch of farmland in the distance. The farther out of the city they drove, the more frequent the stretches. "Oh my God, is that a thatched roof?" she exclaimed as they drove by a stone cottage.

"Probably," Linus replied. "They're popular again, I hear."

"Seriously?"

"Don't knock it. A good one will last you a few decades."

She admired the UK for maintaining its quaintness, something she rarely saw in the city. "We have a Berkshire County in Massachusetts, too," she told him. "My parents took us once so we could see the BSO at Tanglewood."

"BSO?"

"Sorry. Boston Symphony Orchestra. Tanglewood is their summer home. I remember thinking how rural the place was. Clearly I didn't understand rural."

Linus chuckled, the vibration filling the small

space. "I hope you're not expecting an orchestra in this Berkshire. You'll be disappointed."

"I'll survive. I'm not much of a music person, anyway. We only went because my sister was performing in the student chorus." Stella had auditioned a few years later but only made alternate.

"Me, either. We had to take piano lessons when we were children," Linus said. "Chopin hasn't recovered."

"From the playing?" Somehow, she suspected Chopin had survived their efforts quite nicely.

"No, from our whining about having to play. Susan was particularly dramatic about it. Then again, her mother was an actress, so she has the drama gene. Oh, sorry," he said when she frowned. "I should have explained. Susan's my half sister."

"I thought you said your father married his secretary."

"That was his third marriage. Susan was a product of marriage number two. Father was what you would call a serial committer."

Interesting. "How many times was he married?"

"Three, but only because he passed away young. If he'd been healthier, I'm sure there would have been at least one or two more." While he spoke breezily, the tone sounded practiced, like a precomposed interview answer.

"No wonder you don't believe in commitment," she replied.

"You sound like Susan when she's playing armchair psychiatrist."

One didn't need to be a psychiatrist to make a connection. Linus's imposed solitude was a third rail that, up until now, Stella had avoided. Partly because she feared if she talked about it, Linus would then bring up New York again. And partly because she didn't like the heavy feeling she got in her stomach whenever she thought of Linus dating.

However, hearing about his father made her curious.

"What do you think about Susan's theory?"

"I don't think. That's my problem."

"And yet you had deep enough thoughts to stop dating. Seems to me, if you were a bastard, you'd have shrugged off what happened to Victoria and carried on."

She watched as he worked through her logic, only to shake his head. "You're basing your thoughts on the new and improved me. Proof that I was right to back off and enter monkdom. Prior to my evolvement, there is no way you and I would be taking a friendly trip to the country. At least not sleeping in separate beds."

"Aren't I the lucky one," she replied.

Are you? a voice asked in her head. His comment had her fighting not to squirm in her seat. Ever since she'd kissed him, her late-night mind had been playing what-if, imagining what might have happened if Linus hadn't pulled away. Inappropriate as the thoughts were, the fantasy— full of tangled limbs and heated kisses—was a tempting one.

Before the image could invade her mind again, she turned her attention to the window. They'd left the highway and were driving deeper into the country. Occasionally the rock walls and hedges were broken up by the appearance of a village. Tiny clusters of Tudor-style buildings with modern window displays. "What do you think? Anything look familiar?" she asked Toffee.

Head resting on her front paw, the cat blinked and went back to sleep.

"Is that a yes or a no?" Linus asked.

"I think it's more an 'I don't care.' She looks quite comfortable, I have to say. Must be used to the trip."

"Agnes did bring her everywhere."

"I can see why. She and I chat all day long."

"You do? About what?"

Stella blushed. Admitting you held long conversations with a cat was akin to saying you had an imaginary friend. "Oh, you know. The weather. Her food. Agnes's inventory." Linus. "The usual."

Linus nodded. "Everyone needs a good sounding board. How is the inventory going?"

Ah, the inventory. "Pretty good. I'm eager to dig into the country house to see what I can't find. I still can't get over how interesting a life Agnes led." In addition to her love life, she bore witness to some major moments in history. "She crossed paths with just about everyone who was anyone, and I swear half of those people gave her gifts."

"She wasn't the queen of British theater for nothing," Linus remarked.

It was funny. Based on the still photographs, Agnes Moreland wasn't a traditionally beautiful woman. Her nose was too long, and she had an overly prominent jaw. There was something about her, though, that captivated.

"I saw one of her movies the other night," she said. *"Sixpence Sunday."*

"Is that the one where she jumps off Tower Bridge?"

"That's the one." Though her role as the suicidal prostitute wasn't the lead, she managed to overshadow everyone every time she was onscreen. "You can see how she became a star."

"Definitely had charisma, she did, even in her eighties."

Explained why Linus had taken a shine to her. They were two of a kind, he and Agnes. He, too, made a room light up when he entered.

"Any more missing objects?" he asked, oblivious to her thoughts. She'd filled him in on her mystery a few weeks ago.

"Nothing so far that I've noticed. Of course, Agnes owned a lot of bric-a-brac she didn't consider valuable enough to list in the addendum. Who knows if any of that's missing?"

"What does Mrs. Churchill think?"

"She doesn't know, either," Stella replied, recalling that awkward conversation. "Neither does Teddy."

"Hmm…"

"What? You think one of them is lying?"

Linus raised and lowered his right shoulder. "Let's just say I wouldn't necessarily trust one of them."

Stella had an idea which one, too. Thing was, why would Teddy steal such minor objects when he had access to the more valuable ones?

"The less expensive ones are easier to sell," Linus replied when she voiced the question out loud.

"Maybe so, but it's not as though he needs the money." As the man had tersely pointed out multiple times during his visit last summer.

Linus didn't look convinced. "What does Peter say?"

"I haven't mentioned it yet," Stella replied. She didn't want to make him think the situation was anything less than one hundred percent under control. "Not until I have a good theory." She didn't want to chance any bad news, or less-than-awesome news for that matter, leaking out. The weekly status updates her parents demanded were difficult enough. The last time Stella brought up her inventory project, the conversation somehow ended up about the best way to leverage the task on her résumé. The actual details of her job didn't really matter.

Except that Stella was really, really enjoying the details.

"Don't worry. You'll figure out an answer before you leave," Linus said.

At first, Stella didn't quite understand, and then she realized she must have sighed out loud. "Thanks for the vote of confidence."

He looked across the seat at her. "I have plenty of confidence in you." The gentleness in his voice wrapped around her insides. When he said things like that, in that voice, her midnight fantasies developed another layer. Unable to stop her face from warming, she turned her head back to the scenery.

Linus tried not to enjoy the blush Stella was trying to hide, but it was difficult. He wasn't so evolved that he didn't enjoy having an effect on a woman.

There was a moment a few miles back when he feared he'd crossed a line. When he said he'd have seduced her in the old days. It was clear from the way her body tensed that the comment made her uncomfortable. Thankfully, he'd reassured her quickly and changed the subject. The last thing he wanted was to cast an awkward pall over the weekend, especially considering how much he valued the invitation.

Stella had no idea, either. No idea what it meant for her to trust his friendship that much. All the more reason not to muck things up with mention of seduction and sharing a bed. If only...

Ever since the night on the Eye, when she'd hugged him—hugged him!—he couldn't stop thinking about the way she felt in his arms. The moment wasn't supposed to be romantic or tender, but dammit, having her pressed against him, her scent clinging to his clothes afterward, had made an impact. Here it was weeks later, and he could still feel the moment. Definitely a test of his resolve.

He stole a look across the car. Stella had her chin propped on her hand as she studied the landscape, her expression contemplative. So serious. Even in jeans and a sweater, she looked all business.

A familiar tightness gripped him. Sometimes, when he looked at her, he couldn't breathe. Too many emotions clogged his chest. Concern, of course. Desire—he'd be lying if he didn't admit to finding her attractive—and others he couldn't name. Or didn't want to.

The GPS told them their street was the next left. "Almost there," he said. "What do you know about the property?"

"Very little," Stella replied. "I meant to go online to see if I could find a photo, but I didn't get the chance. On one document, it's referred to as a country manor and on another, a cottage. In my head I'm picturing a little carriage house kind of thing."

"Maybe." He thought of the sprawling property thirty or so kilometers east that his family used to call their country home. "*Cottage* could mean a variety of things."

Whatever the house was, it certainly had privacy. The property was hidden behind an ancient stone wall and acres of woodland. To gain access, they drove along a narrow road. "Good thing Toffee's over her explorer phase," he remarked. "Lose her in here and you'd never find her. The tree line is ahead. The house should be right over this bend."

As they rounded the corner, the trees broke to reveal a sprawling nineteenth-century hunting lodge.

Stella gasped. "Holy cow. Toffee owns Downton Abbey."

Not quite. By estate standards, the house was small—certainly smaller than the Collier estate—but it was definitely a luxury home. The stone building boasted large arched windows and an intricately carved wooden door. There were multiple chimneys attached, no doubt, to multiple fireplaces. One, in the middle of the house, was happily puffing smoke.

A dark sedan was parked in the drive. "Were you expected?" he asked Stella.

She shook her head. "The estate pays for a cleaning company, but I don't know why they'd light a fire. Can't be that cold in the house."

"Last time I checked, maid services didn't use rental cars," he said, noting the tag on the license plate. There was only one person he could think of who would be using the house.

From the look on Stella's face, she had come to the same conclusion. "Teddy has his own house. Why would he come here?"

"If I were to venture a guess, I would say he fancied a weekend in the country. Does he have visiting privileges?"

"None that I know of," Stella replied. She undid her seat belt. "Would you mind getting Toffee? I'm going to see what's going on."

If Stella had any doubt they'd entered the wrong house, it disappeared as soon as she crossed the threshold. A giant portrait of a younger Agnes greeted them in the entranceway. The house itself was cozy and rustic with its faded floral wallpaper and antique furniture.

"Bit like walking into a grandma's house," Linus remarked, "if your grandma was a dowager duchess." He set the carrier on a nearby bench and let Toffee free. The cat stretched and began sniffing her surroundings.

"What do you think, Toffee? Smell like home?" he asked.

Leaving them to their conversation, Stella walked a little deeper into the house. Soft music was coming from the room behind the staircase. "Hello," she called out.

"I beg your pardon, but this is private… Oh!" With a tumbler in one hand, and a newspaper tucked under his arm, Teddy Moreland rounded the corner and stopped. He looked dressed for the weekend, a maroon sweater-vest buttoned over his stomach. The color matched the blotches on his cheeks.

He looked at her with wide eyes. "Miss Russo, what a surprise."

"I could say the same, Mr. Moreland. Toffee and I are here to check out the property."

"You brought Etonia Toffee Pudding? All the way from London?"

"Why not? It is her house." They'd had this conversation before.

As if on cue, Toffee jumped off the bench and began weaving between her legs. Stella scooped the cat up to cuddle her. "Besides, I couldn't very well leave her unattended for the weekend, could I?" she added.

"You're staying for the weekend? All of you?"

Teddy's second question was directed at Linus, who had appeared at her shoulder. The insinuation was clear.

"I had the car," Linus answered, without missing a beat. "Since Stella isn't familiar with directions or driving on the left side of the road yet, I offered to play chauffeur."

A slight rearranging of facts, but Stella wasn't about to correct him, especially as the truth only added fuel to Teddy's fire. "I'm here to start an inventory of the property," she said. "Might I ask what you're doing here?"

"Keeping an eye on the property," Teddy replied. As if the answer was obvious. He was using the same tone he used during their initial meeting. Imperious and condescending. "I made a habit of coming by on weekends as a favor to Aunt Agnes after she became ill. Now that she's gone, it's the least I can do to make sure her estate remains cared for."

"That's very kind of you." Her gaze slid to the

drink in his hand. "I'm guessing you spend the night as well. To make sure the house looks occupied."

"Naturally. We wouldn't want people thinking it's vacant. Between the memorabilia hounds and common thieves, not to mention vandals…"

She and Linus shared a look. Squatter though he may be, Teddy raised a good point. The house did benefit from being occupied.

She wasn't in the mood to get into a protracted argument, either. "Looks like the three of us will be spending the weekend together, then," she said. "Maybe you can help me locate some of the items on the inventory sheet."

"Splendid. Anything I can do to help." Teddy's smile looked as forced as Stella's felt. "In fact, why don't I take Etonia Toffee Pudding into the study while the two of you bring your bags upstairs. Come here, my lovely." Before Stella could object, he had the white cat tucked in the crook of his elbow. To Toffee's credit, she didn't object. She looked as indifferent as ever. "I'll just bring her into the library to sit on the sofa with me," he said.

"Well, that certainly showed him who's boss, didn't it?" Stella let out a sigh after Teddy and Toffee disappeared around the corner. "I might as well have asked for permission to stay."

"Don't be so hard on yourself," Linus said,

placing a hand on her shoulder. "What were you supposed to do, toss him out? He wouldn't have gone quietly."

"I know, and I wasn't in the mood for a scene." That didn't change the fact she felt as though she'd messed up.

"Look, you let him know that you're on to him. Chances are, he'll be less inclined to make himself at home in the future. Especially if you drop a few a hints about returning."

While she'd been talking with Teddy, Linus had brought in their luggage, along with Toffee's travel bag. "Are you sure she's staying only for the weekend?" he asked as they headed upstairs.

"I wasn't sure what was here, and I wanted her to be comfortable."

"You know she's going to just sleep on the furniture."

"Well, now she has choices." Sue her for wanting her cat to have choices. Agnes's cat. Toffee.

"You know what irks me the most about the Teddy situation," she said when they reached the second-floor landing. "He's not wrong. It is safer to have someone here once in a while. Not that I buy for a second that's the reason he's hanging out here." More likely he figured Toffee wouldn't be visiting the place.

She tried to put herself in Teddy's shoes. Annoying as the man was, she felt a little sympathy. Knowing you were second in someone's eyes hurt. Losing out to a cat had to be infuriating.

"Does that mean you're going to let him spend weekends here?" Linus asked.

"Depends. Toffee and I will be traveling this way for a good chunk of the fall. He might decide our company isn't worth the effort. Where do you want to sleep?"

She meant which bedroom, as it was clear Teddy had moved into the master suite. Linus, however, arched his brow, causing her to look away.

"I'll take door number two," he replied with a chuckle.

Leaving her with door number one. The blue room. Everything in the room was a shade of the color, from the sapphire brocade bedspread to the blue toile drapes. Tossing her bag on the bed, she opened what she thought was a closet, only to discover the door connected to Linus's room.

"Sorry."

He was in the middle of peeling off his sweater. The sport shirt underneath had ridden up halfway, exposing his torso. She knew he was well built, but this was the first time she'd seen his bare skin. Her eyes followed the dusting of blond hair running from below his navel to where it disappeared beneath his belt.

"I thought this was a closet. I'll…um…give you your privacy."

He freed his head, his hair mussed with static electricity. Seeing her, he smiled. "No worries. I was getting warm, is all. Thought I'd change into a T-shirt. You can leave the door open. That is, unless you want privacy yourself to…"

"No. That is, I'm going to stay dressed. In these clothes."

"Suit yourself. These old houses can get very dusty." With that, he removed his shirt as well.

Stella always thought it a cliché when people said their mouths ran dry, but the sight of a shirtless Linus Collier had her swallowing several times to moisten her throat.

Focus on work, Stella.

"What?" He tipped his head. "Did you say something?"

Damn. "I said I'm going to get to work. Unpacking can wait until later." Much later.

CHAPTER SEVEN

AFTER CHECKING ON TOFFEE, who, to her surprise, was happily stretched out on the back of the sofa behind Teddy, Stella hid herself in the attic. Steamer trunks and boxes made for the perfect distraction, or so she hoped. Stella had a suspicion she'd be haunted by that strip of skin for quite a while.

Why, though? She was never the kind of woman who craved sex. Liked it, sure, but she never ached for physical connection. Now, here she was having fantasies and getting flushed over the sight of a man's treasure trail.

Not any man's. Linus's. Her insides went end over end.

Wasn't this just like her? It really was as though she had a subconscious need for self-sabotage. Why else would she develop a thing for the one man in England who wasn't interested in dating. To top it off, she shouldn't be developing a thing, period.

"Save me, Agnes," she said as she flipped the latch of a footlocker. "Distract me with your memorabilia."

Agnes obliged. Sort of. The footlocker turned out to be a stash of journals and photographs. Not the Limoges pieces Stella was supposed to find, but far more interesting.

Two hours went by before she realized.

"I come with tea."

The voice came out of nowhere. Dropping the stack of photographs she held, Stella clutched her hand to her chest and turned around. Linus stood in the attic doorway, his silhouette backlit by the stairway light.

"Sorry," he said. "Didn't mean to make you jump. I thought you could do with something warm. These old attics can be drafty."

"I hadn't noticed," she replied, her heart rate slowing to normal, "but now that you mention it, I do feel a chill. Thank you."

He came all the way into the room and handed her one of the two earthenware mugs he was carrying. Steam and the aroma of black tea drifted into Stella's face. She inhaled deeply before taking a sip.

"So what is it that has you so engrossed that you didn't notice the temperature?" Linus arranged himself atop the steamer trunk a few feet from her, using a smaller box as a footrest, and cradled his mug. The sloping roof and small space made his presence seem even larger. He was wearing a T-shirt. A gray cotton reminder of earlier.

Suddenly, Stella didn't need the tea for warmth. She sipped it anyway, for something to do. "I found another collection of old photographs. Personal ones this time." The pile she'd dropped lay scattered at her feet. Bending over, she sorted through until she found the one she was looking for. "This looks like it was taken on someone's yacht. Check it out."

Linus whistled. "Is this who I think it is?"

"Read the back. There are journals, too," she added when he arched his brow. "I couldn't stop reading. It's like a giant Pandora's box of awesomeness. The more I read, the more amazed I am." A woman who carved out her life on her terms, that's who Agnes Moreland was. Stella was inadequate in comparison.

Before the dissatisfaction could ruin her mood, she switched topics. "How was your afternoon?

"Quite pleasant. I watched rugby and read a few lab reports and Teddy fell asleep reading the paper. He snores, by the way."

"And Toffee?"

"When I last left her, the owner of the house was batting a piece of uncooked pasta around the kitchen. Do not ask me where she got it."

From the mischievous glint in his eye, Stella

could guess. "Thank you for entertaining her," she said.

It dawned on her that while she'd packed for Toffee, she'd invited Linus along without a single thought as to his entertainment. "I'm a terrible hostess," she said. "I've been ignoring you all afternoon."

"I knew what I was getting into."

And he said yes anyway? A little piece of her melted. "You're a good friend," she said. A reminder for them both. Mostly her, though, since she was also thinking how amazing he was at the moment and how nicely he filled out his T-shirt.

He smiled in response, causing her to smile back, and for several minutes the two of them just sat there smiling.

Linus was the one to break the mood. "That reminds me," he said. "The other reason I came upstairs. Teddy has volunteered to watch Toffee so we could go out to dinner."

"He did?" A frisson of suspicion passed through her. "Why?" Teddy didn't seem the type to make magnanimous gestures.

"We were talking about the Rose and Badger, and I mentioned that I hadn't been there in years but that you don't like to leave Toffee home alone, so he offered. My guess is he wants to win your favor, since you caught him staying here," he added before raising his mug.

"And what is the Rose and Badger?"

"A pub a few kilometers north of here, near the henge. Serves the most amazing roast beef and pudding. My grandfather used to bring us when I was a little boy."

"Did you say *henge*?"

"I did. There's a large one in Avebury. Not as famous as Stonehenge, but very popular with the pagan community. Are you interested? In dinner, I mean."

Dinner with Linus in an authentic English pub across from a pagan henge? Sounded...romantic.

"I had planned to work most of the night." Soon as she answered, she realized how rude that sounded. "I'm also filthy. I've been digging through these dusty papers."

"You look fine. We're talking about a pub, not a five-star restaurant."

"But I packed dinner. Mrs. Churchill made a giant casserole. I put it in the cooler."

He frowned. "What cooler?"

"Sorry. The hamper."

"I know what a cooler is. I was asking what cooler."

"The blue one. I set it next to Toffee's bag."

Linus shook his head. "I unpacked everything from the car. There was no cooler, or whatever you want to call it."

"Sure there is. I distinctly remember putting

the casserole in it. Don't tell me we forgot to pack it?"

"Sorry, luv." He offered her a contrite smile. "Sure you don't want to change your mind about the pub? Least you can do after ignoring me all afternoon."

"You..." He was joking. Nevertheless, his teasing hit a nerve. Stella sighed. She'd hoped to use tonight to make up the time she wasted this afternoon. On the other hand, it was only dinner, and she did owe Linus something for driving.

As for the night sounding romantic...? Romance was ninety-nine percent mental. Linus by candlelight didn't have to be any different than the Linus she saw every day.

"Sure," she replied. "Dinner it is."

The relief Linus felt at Stella's acceptance surprised him, although not nearly as much as the tremor of excitement accompanying it. Taking Stella to dinner wasn't something he'd considered until Teddy mentioned the pub in passing. As soon as he did, though, Linus seized on the opportunity. It would be a complete waste for Stella to work the entire weekend—and she would, too, using Toffee as the excuse. Therefore he immediately began dropping hints until Teddy found himself "volunteering" his cat-sitting services.

Linus told himself the night out was for Stella's sake, and he played off his excitement as satisfaction that his plan worked.

At least he did until dinner. He was in the front entranceway talking with Teddy when he heard Stella descending the stairs.

"I didn't keep you waiting, did I?" she asked.

Dear Lord. All that talk about stopping a room with her entrance... Linus glanced at the portrait on the wall and mentally shook his head. Not even close.

How could Stella not see her own charisma? She'd changed clothes, switching her turtleneck to a V-neck sweater that reflected pink onto her skin. Wide and boxy, the soft-looking knit ended above her waist. Long enough to cover her, but square enough that there was space between sweater and skin. A man could easily slide his hand underneath. The thought affected Linus's ability to breathe.

"Aren't women supposed to make men wait? Aunt Agnes took forever when I was simply visiting for tea."

Thank God for Teddy. Gave him time to clear his throat. "It was worth the wait," he replied. "You look lovely."

She smiled and tucked the hair behind her ear. "I know you said I didn't have to, but after an afternoon in the attic, I needed a shower. Are you sure you don't mind watching Toffee?" she asked, turning to Teddy.

"My dear girl, Etonia Toffee Pudding is like family. I've spent many hours with her sitting near me. Tonight won't be any different."

"We'll only be gone a couple hours," Linus told him.

"Or less," Stella quickly added.

He hated how she was already shortchanging her enjoyment by planning to hurry back.

The Rose and Badger stood on the outskirts of town, on a road leading to Avebury proper. Linus had never given it much thought before, but once upon a time, the pub must have been an inn for Travelers. The building itself was white stucco with thick brown shutters. Above the faded white lettering on the sign was a painting of a badger, a rose trapped beneath its front paws. Sometime during the afternoon, the clouds had receded, leaving behind a full moon. It cast a silvery glow on the parking lot.

"Do you know how pubs got their odd names?" he asked as they stepped out onto the gravel. "The pictures were for illiterate travelers. If you were meeting someone and couldn't read, you could locate an establishment by describing the picture. 'Meet me at the Rose and Badger pub.'"

"Interesting."

Linus winced. He sounded more like a tour guide than a dinner companion. He was out of his element. Normally he took his dates out in the city, where he could charm them with witty anecdotes. This was the first time he'd taken a woman to a place from his childhood.

It also wasn't a date, he reminded himself as he opened the front door.

"I'm going to go out on a limb and say not many pubs were named after their owners then. Unless they knew a professional artist," Stella said, still on his original comment.

"No, but there are a few Slaughtered Lambs and what not."

"Sounds appetizing. Oh, this is lovely."

Not as lovely as her enchanted expression. The pub's interior hadn't changed much since he was a boy, or in the last four hundred years, for that matter. The room was still dark, the light limited to a handful of hanging lanterns and candles on the tables. The same antique farm implements from around the area hung on the exposed beams. At this point Linus almost suspected they were original furnishings, like the pagan symbols interspersed among them.

The air around them smelled of wood smoke, fennel and onion. As they walked to a table near the fireplace, he breathed in the aroma and decided his ruse definitely was worth it. "Admit it," he said. "This is better than reheated casserole."

"Out of respect for Mrs. Churchill, I refuse to comment until I've actually tasted the food. However, I'll admit the atmosphere is impressive."

Why, then, wasn't she relaxed? He could see the tension in her shoulders. Come to think of it, she'd been tense when he first made the suggestion of dinner as well. "If you're worried about staying out too long..." he started.

"It still seems odd that Teddy would volunteer to cat sit. When he came to the apartment, he was all about being served."

"That was before, though. Like I said earlier, maybe he feels the need to get on your good side." Stella shrugged, not quite convinced.

"If you're worried, we can go back."

She looked about to speak, only to stop and shake her head. "No. We're here. And I'm being overprotective, or under-trusting or whatever. I'm sure Toffee will be fine."

Linus let out the breath he hadn't realized he'd been holding. "I fed her before we left. She'll probably spend the night bathing and sleeping by the fire. In fact, I imagine both of them will. Sleep by the fire, that is. I'd rather not picture Teddy licking himself."

"Oh my," Stella said, pressing a hand to her mouth. "Me neither."

They shared a mutual shudder. In the candle-light, Stella's eyes took on a golden sheen. Linus had never paid close attention to a woman's eye color before. He limited himself to three basic descriptors: brown, hazel and blue. Stella's eyes, however, were multidimensional. Multiple shades of brown blended together. A man could stare into them for hours and not be able to pick out all the different colors.

She looked away, and he felt her gaze's absence. "How old did you say this restaurant is?" she asked as she studied the fireplace mantel.

He wanted to catch her chin and turn her face back to his. "Four hundred years. Give or take a few decades."

"Wow. Can you imagine? Four centuries ago, another pair of travelers ate in this very spot."

A fanciful thought. He liked the dreamlike expression it brought to her face. "Maybe. Bet they didn't have as good a wine list, though." He winked at her over the menu.

Get a grip on yourself, Russo. Stella raised the menu in front of her face so Linus couldn't see the blush on her cheeks. What was with her? You'd think she was a nervous teenager on her first date. All day long, her insides had been fluttering and tumbling like someone replaced her organs with a giant swarm of butterflies. It was embarrass-

ing. Right up there with how she took thirty minutes to change her sweater. At least showering
and redoing her makeup made sense after being
in the attic all day. Blushing at every little thing
her friend said did not.

Gosh, but he looked good in candlelight. The
flame brought out the blue in his eyes. Thank
goodness for the menu or she'd lose herself in
them.

The meal passed in a blur of conversation.
Linus entertained her with stories of his childhood. So different from hers. Linus and his
brother were clearly close, as evidenced by the
antics they got into. Even Susan, the so-called
outsider, was involved in some of the adventures.

One obvious thing was the role tradition played
in their upbringing. Colliers was more than a family business. It was the family identity.

"Did it ever occur to you to do something different? Work someplace else?"

"Of course. We all did. Thomas even went
north and played carpenter for a few years.
Grandfather may have talked our ear off about
legacy, but we were always free to go someplace
else if that's what we wanted. It's only by sheer
luck that I happened to love chemistry."

"Your family wouldn't have cared if you decided to design women's shoes or become a
barista instead?"

He thought for a moment before answering. "Hard to say. Father was devastated when Thomas didn't join the company straight off, but he was the heir apparent. But Susan and me? I don't think so. Not if that's what I really wanted to do."

"You're lucky," Stella replied. He was free to be himself.

"Let's talk about something else." She pushed her Cabernet aside. Once again, she'd let the alcohol go to her head and started saying stupid things. "Is there really a henge nearby?"

A look passed over Linus's face, but if he thought her behavior abrupt, he didn't say so. "Across the street. Been here longer than the pub."

"I remember watching a cable show about Stonehenge when I was a kid. About all the mysticism and supernatural theories surrounding it, like how it'd been built by aliens."

He laughed. "We were all about those stories when we were kids as well. Some of the locals still believe them, at least the mysticism part. Why do you think there are herbs everywhere?"

Sitting in the middle of their table was a bud vase with a sprig of dried flowers. Linus reached across and gave the stem a gentle touch with his finger. "Did you know that some people believe lavender can be used to attract love and happiness?"

"Really?" What a nice thought. "You don't?"

"I think the plant has a very pleasant scent and that your olfactory sense reacts in very specific ways to different smells."

"Spoken like a true scientist."

"If the shoe fits," he replied with a smile. "My siblings are the fanciful ones."

"Really?"

"Oh yeah. Thomas and his wife are convinced they were touched by some kind of magical influence." For the next few minutes, he told her about their miraculous reunion following his sister-in-law's accident.

"Your brother really didn't know she was alive?"

"And Rosalind really had amnesia," Linus replied. "Talk to the two of them, and they'll insist Christmas magic was at play. For that matter, my sister, Susan, will tell you the same thing about her romance."

"While you have no magic at all. Poor baby." She was only half joking. While she didn't believe in magic any more than Linus did, it bothered her that he was the odd man out.

"I'll survive," he said with a wave of his hand. "I don't need to turn basic coincidence into anything deeper."

Maybe not, but what about feelings in general? While his siblings were falling in love, he was swearing off the emotion. The thought left her with an empty feeling. He deserved love as much as anyone. Without giving it a second thought, Stella covered his hand with hers—the way any friend comforting another friend would.

"You might not need to, but you deserve the chance anyway," she said.

Linus stared at their hands for a second before rotating his so that their palms touched and gently closed his fingers around hers.

When his thumb rubbed the outside of her little finger, Stella felt the touch all the way to her toes. If he were to lean across and kiss her right now, she would...

"Hey, come with me." His voice broke her thought. "I want to show you something outside."

They left the restaurant and went across the street. The night was quiet. With each step they took deeper into the field, the farther the sounds from the pub receded until eventually the only noises they could hear were their footsteps in the grass and the occasional snap of an animal in the brush. The full moon was like a giant silver lantern making it easy to see the outlines of the ancient stone rocks that formed the circle. What the moon couldn't illuminate, the flashlight on Linus's phone did. He kept the light trained on the ground so they wouldn't lose their footing.

As she walked along, Stella could see why people found the site special. The air definitely felt charged with something. Like a sense of anticipation.

"Where are we were going?" she asked. "You're not offering me up as a sacrifice, are you?"

"Depends. Are you a virgin?" He gave her hand a squeeze.

They had been holding hands since the restaurant. Linus claimed it was to keep her from stumbling. Stella didn't care. Jokes about sacrifice aside, she found his grip reassuring.

"Seriously?" she asked. "We've passed at least a half dozen of those large rocks. What is it we're looking for?"

"It's a surprise. At least I hope it will be. Hopefully it still exists."

Again, Stella didn't care. The wine, the air, the hand in hers were enough.

They walked awhile longer in comfortable silence. Then suddenly, Linus spoke. "Ah, here we are. Watch your step."

It was a large tree in a nearby gully. Although they were buried by leaves, Stella could see bits and pieces of the root system as it spread across the ground like giant tentacles. Considering the roots' size and range, the tree had to be ancient. "It's a beech tree," Linus said. "There are only a handful of them around. Supposed to have mystical properties. At least particular ones."

Letting go of her hand, he stepped behind her

and shone the light upward. Stella gasped. Ribbons of every color and size adorned the branches. Some were old and tattered, others new.

"What are the ribbons for?" she asked.

"Wishes and desires."

"Like a wishing well, only with branches and ribbons."

"Precisely. I'd forgotten about it until you mentioned magic."

Stella watched the ribbons moved in the breeze. With the moon overhead and the silhouettes of monoliths behind them, the branches looked almost otherworldly.

She tilted her head farther back, even though it strained her neck. Linus was gazing upward, too. "Did you ever make a wish and tie a ribbon?"

"Once, when we were kids."

"Do you remember what you wished for?"

"Probably a chemistry set or to be a starter on the football team. Something that seemed very important at the time, I'm sure."

The wishes of children. Stella tried to imagine Linus as a little boy with little-boy dreams. "I'm sure I'd have wished for something equally earth-shattering." She thought of all the times she'd tossed pennies into fountains with the hopes she'd be as good as her siblings at some endeavor.

"I'm sorry I don't have any ribbons or we could leave a wish right now."

"That's all right." The pennies never worked; why would a ribbon? Although she was curious. "What would you wish for if we did have ribbons?"

"Me?" She felt him shrug. "A new chemistry set?"

"Seriously," she replied. Even if she didn't believe in wishes, the surroundings called for honesty. She knew what she'd wish for, for him.

His ensuing silence lasted for so long, she was afraid he wasn't going to answer. Finally, in a soft voice, he said, "I would wish to be better. A better brother. A better person. Just better."

Oh, Linus. What he should wish for was the ability to forgive himself. As far as Stella was concerned, he was good enough as is.

"What about you?" he asked. "What is your heart's desire?"

To know my heart's desire.

The thought sounded clear and loud in her head. Stella pushed it aside. The thought didn't even make sense. "To be happy," she said instead. Again, the thought came out of nowhere. What she should have said was "to become a major player in the world financial market." Something concrete and in keeping with her goals. Wishing for happiness was as nebulous as wishing for peace on earth.

She started to clarify herself when Linus's hand

settled on the back of her neck. Cold skin met cold skin, sending warm shivers down her back. Her knees very nearly buckled. "I hope you get your wish," he said. "I want you to be happy, too."

And then he kissed the top of her head.

They walked back in silence. Linus didn't hold her hand this time. He wanted to, but after their interlude under the tree, signs of affection felt presumptuous. Especially since his initial answer to Stella's question had been "you." He would wish for Stella, in his arms. Exactly the kind of wish he had no business making for a number of reasons. Starting with the fact that she needed a friend, not an affair. And so he wished to be better, because better was what he needed to be.

Even though what he wanted was to kiss her until she couldn't breathe. He licked his lips and imagined the taste of her. Imagination: the price of being better.

Stella finally broke the silence in the car, a half kilometer from home. Until then, she'd stared out the window with a faraway look on her face.

"Thank you for a wonderful evening," she said. "I'm glad you talked me into going."

"I'm glad you enjoyed yourself." It struck him just how much satisfaction he gotten out of the evening. Making Stella smile gave him a rush, not dissimilar to the thrill he used to get from the chase, only he wasn't looking to gain anything further from the outcome.

"Don't tell Mrs. Churchill, but I'm glad we forgot her casserole in London."

The casserole. He'd pushed that part of the evening out of his head. Did he want to ruin such a good evening? "About that…" Might as well tear the bandage off now. She was going to find out regardless. "I'm afraid I might have fibbed a bit."

"Fibbed how?" she asked. Her eyes narrowed.

"The cooler. It might be in the kitchen back at the house."

"You lied?"

He preferred to think he misrepresented the truth for a greater good. "Only when it was obvious you weren't going to say yes otherwise. And I really wanted to take you out this evening."

Stella huffed and folded her arms. "I don't like being lied to."

"I'm sorry, but I meant what I said. I only lied when I realized you weren't going to say yes unless backed into a corner. If I hadn't, you'd have spent the night up in the attic and left me to hang with Teddy."

"Don't try to guilt me," she said.

"I wasn't trying to make you feel anything." Perhaps he was trying for a little guilt, but she couldn't say he wasn't speaking the truth. She would have worked all night. "I lied because I wanted to spend some time with you, pure and simple."

"You could have just told me. You didn't have to play games."

"Would that have changed your mind?"

Stella didn't answer. In the dark, it was impossible to see her expression, but Linus imagined her jaw to be tensed.

Way to go, Collier. First real female friendship he'd ever had, and he'd mucked it all up. Why didn't he come out and say he wanted to spend time with her?

Because then it would feel too much like asking her on a date, that's why. He didn't want her to feel that kind of pressure.

Or was he simply afraid she'd say no?

CHAPTER EIGHT

THE FRONT OF the house was dark when he parked the car, including the exterior lights. Only a glow coming through from the rear of the house indicated anyone was home.

The car engine had barely stopped when Stella threw open the passenger door. "I'm going to get Toffee and head to bed."

"Stella, wait…"

She shut the door on his sentence.

Fortunately, the front door was unlocked. They let themselves in, and Linus felt along the wall until he found the switch. "Teddy? We're back."

There was no answer.

"Looks like someone fell asleep in front of the telly," he said. Or passed out. A daylong diet of gin and tonics could do that to a person.

Still bent on ignoring him, Stella marched off in the direction of the library. Linus headed toward the stairway. No sense trying to talk tonight. He'd wait until she got a good night's sleep, as well as a few hours' work under her belt, and then he'd talk to her. Maybe—hopefully—by the end of their drive home, things would be back to normal. If not... His stomach grew heavy.

He had one foot on the stair when Stella's voice cut through the house.

"What the hell do you think you're doing?"

Stella entered the library in time to see Teddy crouched in front of an open French door. At the sound of her voice, he jumped up, Toffee clutched to his chest. The cat reacted to the sudden movement by scrambling up and over his shoulder, landing on the sofa before running full speed out of the room.

"That was almost a disaster," Teddy said. "Thank goodness she ran down the hall. You should know better than to holler like a banshee, Miss Russo."

"Excuse me?" *She* should know better? He was the one she'd caught standing in front of the open door.

Linus came running down the hall. "What's going on? I heard Stella yell, and then the cat nearly tripped me trying to run upstairs."

"I caught Teddy here trying to put Toffee outside," Stella told him.

Teddy's nostrils flared. "I did nothing of the sort."

"I saw you crouching in the doorway. What was the plan?" she asked as she shut the door.

"Put her out in the woods and hope she got lost for good? Maybe get eaten by a badger?" With Toffee lost in the woods, he would be the heir.

She knew she should have stayed home.

"How dare you! What kind of man do you think I am?"

"A person who stands to inherit eleven million pounds if Toffee disappears," Linus said.

"I don't need your help," Stella said. It was partly his fault Teddy was alone with Toffee in the first place. If having dinner with him hadn't sounded so appealing...

"For your information, I was protecting Etonia Toffee Pudding. She very nearly got outside," Teddy said.

"And why was the door open in the first place?" Stella asked. He couldn't fool her. The man was trying to shoo Toffee outside hoping she'd get lost in the woods. One lost cat would mean payday for him.

"Earlier in the evening, there was an issue with the fire, and the room became smoky. I opened the door a crack to air the room out. You remember, Collier. You were with me."

Stella looked at Linus. He gave her a sheepish nod. "He's right. There was a backdraft."

"Unfortunately, the door must not have latched tightly when I closed it, and it blew open with the wind. Thankfully, I was coming in to turn out the lights when I saw Etonia Toffee Pudding sniffing the ground outside. I had just managed to lure her in when you screamed like a banshee, scaring us all."

When he finished, Teddy stood and waited for her apology, arms folded across his midsection. There was a pull in his sweater from where Toffee had climbed over his shoulder. Stella was willing to bet there was a good long scratch on the skin beneath as well.

"What was Toffee doing in a room with an open door?" she asked.

"Well, it certainly wasn't my fault. She was sleeping on the sofa when I started my rounds." Should she believe him? She'd already been lied to once this evening, and quite believably. Teddy could be lying to her as well.

On the other hand, Teddy's story made sense. And, Toffee had a history of sneaking outside when no one was looking. Witness her visit to Linus's house this summer. And even if Teddy was lying, Stella had no proof other than her gut.

"I'm sorry, Teddy. Forgive me." As much as it galled her to apologize, she had to coexist with the man for the rest of her tenure. She couldn't afford to get on his bad side. "I'm extremely protective of Toffee, as you can see, and that sometimes leads me to jump to the worst-case scenario. Thank you for making sure Toffee was safe."

"Well..." The older man made a production out of checking his cuffs. "It is important that the cat be protected at all costs. I should be grateful that you're taking your job as seriously as you are. Therefore, I accept your apology."

"Thank you," Stella replied. "Now if you'll excuse me, I'm going to find Toffee and get some sleep."

"Do you think he's telling the truth?" Linus asked when they were on their way upstairs.

"You tell me. I'm not very good at sussing out lies these days." She was still annoyed at him, too.

Part of her felt like she was overreacting to the whole thing with the cooler. A casserole was hardly life or death. But it wasn't what he'd lied about that had her angry; it was that he'd played her, like she imagined he'd played countless other women. She'd thought she was different.

She wanted to be different.

And there was the real source of her annoyance. She was upset because she'd allowed herself to fall under the night's spell. To think that what they were sharing in Avebury was special.

She didn't bother waiting to hear Linus's answer about Teddy. When they reached the top of the stairs, she went straight to the master bedroom to look under the bed, figuring Toffee would hide in a familiar place. She was wrong. After checking the room thoroughly—if Teddy whined about invasion of privacy, he could stuff it—she headed to her own room.

Linus sat on the bed, fluffy white cat in his lap. "Peace offering," he said. "Found her sitting next to my pillow. She doesn't seem too traumatized."

"Well, that's good." She stroked the cat's head. "Sorry I scared you, sweetie."

"I'm sorry, too," Linus said. "For the bit about the cooler. I should have straight-out said I wanted to take you to dinner. Truth is, I was afraid."

"That I would take it the wrong way."

He looked her in the eye. "That you would say no."

Oh.

"In case you haven't guessed, I like your company," he continued. "I like…spending time with you."

"I like…spending time with you, too." More than she should, really. "In fact, you're the only person who's ever been able to drag me away from a project."

"Really?"

"Don't let it go to your head." She sat down on the bed next to him. "I'm glad we went out tonight. It was really…" *Special*, she wanted to say. "Nice."

"Yeah, it was. I meant what I said, too, in Avebury. I want you to be happy."

Stella's breath caught in her throat. Linus's gaze was dark and unshuttered, revealing the vulnerability within. When was the last time a man had looked at her with such sincerity? Ever? The emotion set off a heavy heat deep inside her. She felt special. Wanted.

They were friends. Good friends. But suddenly friendship wasn't enough. Her body wanted more. Needed more.

She began to lean forward, then caught herself. The last time she'd kissed him, he'd pushed her away. She wouldn't repeat the mistake.

"I should leave," Linus said. "Before I do something we regret."

"Would we?" Stella asked. "Regret it?"

"We're friends."

"Friends can have benefits."

She waited, watching as his eyes dropped to her mouth. The ache inside her had intensified. *Please*, she pleaded silently. *Please.*

"I don't want to…"

"You won't," she said. "I know what I'm asking. This won't change anything."

Something flickered in his expression, but it moved too quickly for her to catch. There was no time to think about it anyway, because a moment later he was kissing her. Slowly. Deeply. His fingers tangling in her hair.

There was a soft thud that she realized was

Toffee jumping to the floor. It was the last she thought of the cat as she sank into the mattress, Linus's body atop hers.

"Does this mean I'm forgiven?"

Linus laughed and tightened his embrace as Stella gave him a playful shove in the shoulder. This, pressed chest to chest in the sheets of Stella's bed, was the last place he imagined he'd be when he left London this morning. Hell, it was the last place he'd imagined an hour ago.

What an hour, though.

"This won't change anything."

Stella's words drifted into his post-lovemaking haze. Her attempt at reassurance. That they would still be friends. Friends with benefits. No expectations. No misreading of intentions.

Why did that bother him?

"Hey. Where'd you go?" Stella's gentle voice lured him back to the present.

"Nowhere important." He brushed the bangs from her face. Her skin still bore a hint of flush. Stella pink. His new favorite color.

"Was thinking how nice this feels. Never expected to end up here."

"Mmm…" Giving a little purr, she began to nuzzle closer only to pause and pull back. "It's good, though?"

The doubt in her voice broke his heart. How

on earth could she think otherwise? "Very." He pressed his lips to her shoulder to emphasize the point.

"Good." This time she tucked her head under his chin without pause.

They lay that way for a while, Linus's fingers tracing a lazy trail up and down Stella's spine. There was a soft meow, and a few seconds later a weight landed on the bed and began to purr.

"Why yes, Toffee, we'd love if you'd join us," he said.

Stella giggled. "As far as she's concerned, you're the interloper. Her house, remember?"

"True. Although in fairness, she would assume she owned any house she was in as a matter of feline privilege. Isn't that right, Toffee?" Proving his point, the cat plopped down against his leg.

"Do you think Teddy was telling the truth?" He'd prefer not to think of Teddy at all under the circumstances.

"I don't know. Like I said, it's a plausible story. We have no way of proving he isn't telling the truth."

"You're right. I suppose even if he was lying, there's not much we can do now. We'll be back to London tomorrow, and I'll make sure he's never alone with Toffee again."

"So much for late-night walks in Avebury," he muttered.

"Not unless we bring her along."

"Wouldn't that make an interesting picture. The two of us hauling a pet carrier in the moonlight." He smiled at the image.

Closing his eyes, he listened to the synchronized rhythm of their breaths. Each rise and fall reminding him of waves crashing against the shore. Little by little, he felt himself being pulled toward sleep.

"I meant what I said," Stella said suddenly.

"About what?" In his dreamlike state, his brain was slow to comprehend. Was she talking about Toffee still?

"About this not having to change anything."

He was awake now, a heaviness filling his stomach. "It won't?"

"No, so you don't have to worry about my freaking out or wonder if you're hurting me. Because I don't have any expectations. I promise."

"That's... Okay." Of course she didn't have expectations, as she'd made it clear time and again that any kind of emotional entanglement wasn't part of her plan. And as someone who'd vowed the same, he should be relieved.

Why, then, was he disappointed?

CHAPTER NINE

Winter

LINUS STARED AT the brightly wrapped package in his hand. Inside was a gold chain with a tiny gold charm shaped like a ribbon. He knew because he'd spent an afternoon debating whether he should buy the bloody thing. A week later, he still wasn't sure.

"You're wasting your time, Linus, old man."

Linus stashed the box in his jacket pocket just before his brother, Thomas, clapped him on the shoulder. The normally staid executive was wearing the most garish Christmas sweater known to man and was munching on a Christmas cookie.

"Christmas Eve was last night," he said. "You're going to have to wait a whole three hundred and sixty-five days if you want to catch Santa."

Linus forced a smile. "Figured it was worth a try. Seeing as how you all have a special Christmas connection. Kids asleep?"

"Just about. Maddie crashed before I finished reading her first bedtime story. Rosalind's tucking in Noel. Who's the present for?"

"What present?"

"The one you just hid in your pocket," Thomas replied.

"Oh, that present. It's nothing. Just something I bought for a friend."

His brother took a bite of cookie. "This friend wouldn't be your pet-sitting neighbor, by any chance?"

"Estate manager." The correction was automatic. Linus swore his siblings purposely used the wrong title to bother him. Turning from the fireplace—and his brother—he headed to the other side of the living room, where Thomas had placed the bar.

"I'll take that as a yes," Thomas replied. "Hardly a surprise. She's the only person you socialize with outside of family. Why all the fuss?"

"Because I haven't decided if I want to give it to her," Linus replied. "Are you out of Scotch?"

"Bottom shelf, and why not?"

For a host of reasons, starting with whether Stella would consider the gift too extravagant—or worse, too sentimental. So uncertain was he that he'd even bought a backup present.

"I'm not sure, is all. We didn't talk about exchanging gifts. I don't want to put her on the spot."

In the past, if he was dating someone at Christmastime, he bought her something sparkly. But Stella wasn't the "something sparkly" type. Nor were they dating. They were "without expectations."

Stella had been right about one thing. When they returned from the country, things didn't change. They continued much as they had before, except that Linus slept over once or twice a week. She didn't ask where their relationship was going or talk about the future. She didn't ask him to share anything but her bed. If the two of them stopped sleeping together tomorrow, they would probably carry on. It was the perfect no-guilt affair. And yet, for the past six weeks, he'd been growing more and more unsettled.

He poured two glasses and handed one to Thomas. "The ice is melted. You'll have to drink it neat."

"I didn't realize I was drinking," he replied.

"I don't feel like drinking alone." Linus let the alcohol slide down his throat, savoring its warm burn. "That's how good Scotch should taste. Merry Christmas," he said.

"Merry Christmas." Thomas mirrored his action before setting the glass down on the bar. "You've been spending a lot of time with your neighbor these days."

"So?"

"So nothing. Glad to see you're getting out

again after that whole Victoria nightmare. Susan said the woman seems very nice."

"Yeah, she's fantastic," Linus replied. The warmth inside him spread up and out, causing him to break out in a smile. "I've never met anyone like her."

Thomas gave him a long look.

"It's not what you think. We're friends. Good friends." He washed the words down with another swallow.

His brother continued to look at him, skepticism evident, so Linus added, "Lady's choice. She wants to keep things casual."

"Ah. Suddenly the present debate makes sense. Never thought I'd see the day when you were more serious than the woman."

"I'm not serious, either," Linus replied. "It's a mutual arrangement."

"Is that why you didn't bring her to Christmas? Whatever your status, I'd hate to think she's alone for the holidays."

"She's not. Her parents are visiting from Boston."

Stella had been high hover about the visit all week. Everything had to be perfect. The gifts, the decorations, the menu. One thing not on the list was her neighbor-slash-lover. She'd insisted he spend the holiday with his family like he always did.

Because she didn't want him feeling obligated, he told himself.

Problem was, he really wanted to see her. It'd been days since they'd spent time together, and he missed her smile.

"I'm debating stopping by on my way home to say merry Christmas. I don't want to intrude. On the other hand, it's the holiday."

Listen to him. He sounded like a lovesick idiot. Was this what it was like for the women he'd dated? This continual vacillating of uncertainty? Clearly, he owed them all apologies.

"Are you sure this is casual, Linus?" Thomas asked. "Because you're not acting like you normally do."

Because Linus didn't feel like he normally did. He didn't want to put a name to the emotions squeezing his chest because then he'd be in real trouble, but his refusal didn't stop the sensation. "Positive. She's out of here in six months. Plans to go back and take the international consulting world by storm."

"Plans can change," his brother replied. "Look at me. Couple years ago I was ready to leave the company for good, remember?"

"Different situation." Thomas had been trying to save his marriage. Stella's goals were about winning her father's pride. "Besides, there's no reason for her plans to change. We're simply having fun in the moment. If anything, it's refreshing to be on the same page with a woman. Much less stress."

"Except for the Christmas gift," Thomas said.

"Except for the Christmas gift." Having finished his drink, he debated pouring a second. Two Scotches felt too much like wallowing in alcohol.

"What did you get her?"

"A reminder of a very special night we shared, and before you say a word, get your mind out of the gutter. I'm referring to the tree in Avebury."

"I have zero idea what you're talking about, but I say go for it. If I've learned anything from being married, it's that women appreciate thoughtful gestures. If you bought something that has meaning, she'll like it." He gave Linus another look, this one using his glass to mask a grin. "Keeping it casual and fun, eh?"

Linus started to rethink that second Scotch.

Stella's sister's face filled half the divided computer screen. She wore a scrub top and a white lab coat.

"I wish I could be there with all of you," she said. "Cafeteria turkey is not the same as Mom's."

"We miss you, too, honey," Kevin Russo said, "but we understand. There'll be plenty of time for you to get away one you're established."

"In the meantime, I'll overnight you a container

of stuffing as soon as we get back to Boston," Rose Russo added.

"What about me?" Her brother's face filled the other half of the screen. "I like your stuffing, too."

"I'll send you both stuffing. And apple pie."

Stella watched the conversation from the ottoman behind her parents. Toffee sat on her lap, the Angora doing her best to mark Stella's skirt with fur. Behind her, Agnes's china was neatly stacked on the dining room table, next to her silverware and glasses. They'd washed everything by hand since her mother was uncomfortable washing borrowed dishes in the dishwasher.

The Russo family video chat had become a tradition as neither Joe nor Camilla could spare time from work to travel. Both her parents took their continued absences in stride. They liked being able to tell people their oh-so-successful children were too important to spare.

This was the year she was supposed to be too important to spare as well.

"How's London?" Camilla was asking.

"Very nice," her mother replied. "Stella's been a wonderful tour guide."

"Guess when your boss is a cat, it's easy to get time off, hey, sis? Just throw a little extra food in the bowl and you're good to go?"

"Catnip," Stella replied. Her smile was tight, but Joe wouldn't notice. "Works every time."

"I thought maybe you had to bring her everywhere like those crazy cat ladies," Camilla said.

"I'm surprised she doesn't," her father said. "You should see the routine this cat has. Food. Brushing. She lives like a queen."

"Guess you should have gone to grooming school instead of studying finance, sis."

"You know, I do more than pet sit," Stella replied. Why did everyone treat her job like it was a joke? "I manage the estate. I'll have you know this cat has a sizable investment portfolio—"

"Which an outside investment company handles," her father cut in.

Yes, but Stella worked closely with them.

Working wasn't the same as doing, her father had been saying all weekend. He'd been saying a lot of things, like how she shouldn't have spent the money on plane tickets, about how she should push for more substantial work. How she shouldn't have signed a one-year agreement. Same script she'd been listening to—and would continue hearing until she returned to Mitchum, Baker.

She would return, though, and next Christmas, she'd be video calling home, too.

"Hey! I almost forgot! Guess who is presenting at the Association of Trial Lawyers midwinter meeting?"

Rose clapped her hands. "Joseph, that's wonderful! Congratulations. Where is the meeting?"

"Miami."

"No way! That's where I'm presenting my paper on odontoid synchondrosis fractures in toddlers. Wouldn't it be a riot if we were there at the same time?"

"You're presenting a paper, too?" Kevin said. "I told you all that work would pay off."

Stella edged away from the conversation. They would be talking about papers and Florida for a while, so no one would notice if she wasn't participating. She looked around her living room. There was a tree in the center, lit with tiny white lights and plastic decorations. Stella thought it odd until she realized Agnes must had purchased decorations with Toffee in mind. She found a box of vintage decorations tucked away in the attic along with a note signed by Larry and Vivien. Every item was another piece in the Dame Agnes Moreland story.

Stella hadn't told anyone, but she'd begun writing Agnes's story using the information in Agnes's letters and journals. Her parents didn't understand the fascination. Every time she tried to tell them, her father would wave off the topic. And Linus…

Without meaning to, she sighed. Linus would encourage her. Like he always did. There was no reason not to tell him. No reason to tell him, either. They didn't have to share everything because they shared a bed.

The best part of her week, the nights with Linus. Took all her restraint not to invite him to stay every night. She was determined to keep her promise and keep things between them casual. The guilt over Victoria was still there; Stella saw it in the shadow that crossed his face whenever he didn't think she was looking. He feared hurting her, and so she worked extra hard to make sure he knew that wouldn't happen. That she didn't expect anything from him beyond what they had.

The job would be a lot easier if she didn't miss him desperately on the nights he wasn't here. All she'd wanted these past couple days was to see his smile over morning coffee.

Sometimes, when they were having breakfast, Stella would look across the table at him, and her chest would feel like it was about to explode with fullness. So much of her life had been spent working toward a goal, on chasing some form of better or more that she could never quite reach. In those moments, though, when she looked at Linus, she didn't need to chase anything. The feeling was addictive and terrifying.

That's why she said no to spending Christmas together. It was clear to her that she was getting a little too attached to Linus. To see him smiling at her from across a family dinner table... God knew what effect that would have on her.

In the other room, she could hear the video chat wrapping up. Not wanting to be rude, she pasted on a smile and went back to say merry Christmas.

"Well, this makes a very merry Christmas indeed," her father said upon ending the call. "Always enjoy hearing the kids' good news. I can't wait to tell Donny. Maybe now he'll stop yapping about Dougie's pediatrics practice."

"Janice will be beside herself," Rose added. "Her daughter has always had a crush on Joe."

"Joe's always had a crush on Joe."

"Did you say something, Stella?"

"No, Mom."

"Those two are really making a mark in this world. I couldn't be prouder. You know what it is? It's because they're focused. They know what they want, and they don't stop until they've achieved it. They don't let a little adversity slow them down."

"No, they don't," Stella said. She added her father's speech to the list of things she'd heard before. Best to simply agree. Anything less would sound defensive, and as her parents were quick to point out, praising her older siblings didn't mean they were slighting her. Except they were.

"Are you expecting someone?" her mother asked when the doorbell rang.

"Not really." Hoping, but not expecting. She could kick herself for the way her pulse quickened. Couldn't she get through a week without needing to see the man?

She could give herself a double kick for the butterflies taking flight in her stomach when she looked through the peephole.

She flung open the door. "Merry Christmas," he greeted.

"Mer—" Before she could finish, he had pulled her into the hall and was kissing her. He tasted like fresh air and peppermint. Needing more, she pressed herself against him, her leg hooking around his in a quest to get closer. They were putting on an indecent show, but she didn't care.

"Merry Christmas yourself," she whispered when they finally parted. "Do you greet everyone who answers their door like that?"

He brushed the hair from her cheek. "Only the really gorgeous ones," he replied. "Can be a bit awkward if their spouse is home."

"Or their parents," she said, untangling herself. Her body protested at losing his warmth. "They're going to wonder what I'm doing outside. This is a very nice surprise. I wasn't expecting you to come by tonight."

"I…" There was that shadow again. The concern she wanted more. "I wanted to wish you a happy Christmas. Doesn't pack quite the same result on December 26."

"No, it does not." It was a struggle not to grab him by the lapels and start kissing again. Stella had no idea how badly she'd missed him—that is, she knew she'd missed him a lot, but she'd had no idea how much a lot really was. It was like a switch inside her had been turned off and his arrival turned it back on.

Not good. Not good at all. She was going to have to do something about her attachment.

"Did you want to come in?" she asked, before quickly adding, "You don't have to stay long. I know it's late, but my parents—well, my mother, really—will want to know who rang the doorbell, so it might help if you stuck your head in and said hello. Nothing big. I'm not expecting you to stay." The last thing she wanted was for him to feel forced into a "meet the parents" scenario.

"Because it's late," he said.

"Exactly, and I'm sure you're tired after chasing your niece around all day."

"Not so tired that I can't step inside for a moment."

"Really?" Could she sound any more eager? "I mean, great."

The two of them stepped inside to discover her parents standing in the center of the living room.

Her mother was holding Toffee. Her father was frowning.

"Everything all right, Stella?" he asked.

When did time revert back to high school? Her parents were staring at her like she'd missed curfew, and her heart was racing like a girl on her first date.

Stella took a deep breath. "Everything is fine. This is my…" She stumbled for the right word. "Neighbor, Linus Collier. He stopped by to say merry Christmas. Linus, these are my parents, Kevin and Rose Russo."

Linus had never met a woman's parents before. Family introductions carried implications. They were a benchmark that implied you were no longer dating, but rather a couple. He and Stella were neither, and yet, he had to wipe his palm on his pants before shaking Stella's father's hand.

Kevin Russo was tall and barrel-chested, with a thick head of silver hair. He had the calloused handshake of a man who worked hard and the cashmere sweater of one who was reaping the benefits. His wife, Rose, looked like an older version of Stella, only with salt-and-pepper hair.

"Merry Christmas," she greeted. "It's nice to meet you. Stella didn't tell us she was friendly with her neighbor."

He didn't even warrant a mention. Linus tried

not to let his disappointment show. "Well, we are the only two people on the floor."

"Linus and I are running partners," Stella explained. "That's how I know my way around London. He's been running me all over the city."

"Bit of a rabbit, she is. I've taken more than a few seconds off my time keeping up."

"Liar," Stella said. "I'm the one working to keep up with him."

They took seats in the living room, Stella's father taking the large chair by the tree. Linus drank in Stella's appearance. She looked magnificent tonight in a black turtleneck and watch plaid skirt. The hem was short enough he could see a glimpse of thigh when she crossed her legs.

"My children are all athletes," Kevin was saying. "Our eldest, Camilla, ran track in college. The four-forty."

"Four hundred meters," Stella supplied.

"Impressive. Good for her." Stella had already told him, along with the fact that she—unlike her sister—didn't run in college.

Meanwhile, Stella caught him checking out her thighs and winked. He wondered what her father would say if he knew that while he was singing his eldest daughter's praises, Linus was thinking about running his hands along the inside of the man's youngest daughter's legs.

"Are you enjoying your trip to London?" he

asked. "I'm guessing Stella has shown you all the highlights."

"Couldn't ask for a better tour guide," Rose replied. No surprise there. Stella had spent the week before their arrival staying awake late into the night, searching for tourist tips. "Of course, Kevin and I have been to London several times, but we liked getting her perspective. It's been nice seeing how she's getting along after… I mean, over here."

"From the looks of things, I'd say she'd doing quite well," Linus said. "At least she seems put together when I see her getting the mail. Are you failing at anything we don't know about?"

"If I am, my lips are sealed." She grinned, and damned if his insides didn't get turned around. He had to cross his legs to keep his arousal at bay.

"Has Stella told you about Dame Agnes's vast collection of memorabilia? The woman was quite a character."

"We guessed that when she left all the money to that one." Rose tipped her head toward Toffee, who was sniffing the Christmas tree branches.

"Creative types. They don't think like the rest of us, do they?" Kevin said. "I always told my kids, make sure you go into something practical like law or medicine."

"Or business," Linus interjected.

"Or business. I never met anyone who made money majoring in history or the arts."

"What do you do for a living, Mr. Collier?" Rose asked.

Linus wanted to tell her a job that involved history or the arts, especially after the way Stella looked down at her hands at her father's comment, but he didn't want to cause an argument. "I'm a chemist."

"See? Science. A good practical major. Camilla, that's Stella's sister, majored in biology. She's a neurosurgeon now."

He went on for several minutes about Stella's siblings and their careers. Good, practical careers. Linus nodded and showed the appropriate appreciation, all the while waiting for the man to get to his youngest.

Across the way he could see Stella folding in on herself, the weight of her father's obliviousness bearing down on her. Her mother was no better. Her attention to her daughter focused on Stella playing the proper hostess. Twice she interrupted to suggest Stella get him coffee or a cocktail.

He wasn't sure he liked the Russos. He didn't care how big the chip on Kevin Russo's shoulder over dropping out of school was.

"Sounds as though you've raised three successful children," he said.

"That's always been my goal," Kevin told him. "To make sure my kids had the chance to accomplish everything I never had the chance to do. Of course," Kevin continued, "Stella's real career is in New York. Corporate finance. She won't be doing this job forever. Isn't that right, sweetheart?"

Stella's smile looked strained as she nodded. At least he didn't call her a pet sitter. He might have been tempted to consider Russo's words a warning about getting serious with his daughter, but he doubted the man thought him a threat. He was too secure in his knowledge that Stella would be returning to New York. To "have the chance" to do everything he hadn't accomplished.

And why shouldn't he be confident? Stella bloody flew them here to impress them.

Meanwhile the man was busy bragging about everyone but her. The man had a beautiful, smart, amazing daughter sitting five feet away, and he couldn't see her. Took all of Linus's willpower not to strangle Kevin Russo's thick neck. Or, at the very least, to tell him to take his aspirations and stuff them.

"Toffee, no!" Stella clapped her hands, startling everyone in the room. She was answered by an annoyed-sounding meow and the tinkling of glass.

"Sorry," she said. "Toffee's obsessed with one

of the bird ornaments on the tree. I caught her trying to climb the branches the other day."

It was the break in the conversation he needed. Linus stood up. "On that note, I think I'll say good-night."

"Do you have to go?" Stella asked.

He both loved and hated the disappointment in her voice. "I'm afraid so. Maddie ran me ragged. My niece," he added for her parents' benefit. "It was a pleasure meeting you both."

Stella walked him to the door. When they were far enough from the living room, she slipped in between him and the door. "Are you too tired for a visitor later?" she asked. "I was hoping to bring by a little Christmas present."

God, but he loved when her voice turned husky. He dropped his gaze to her lips. "I could be persuaded to stay awake for a bit."

"Good. I'll be by as soon as I can."

As she spoke, she ran her finger down his stomach to his belt and crooked a finger into his waistband. Linus sucked in his breath, his head suddenly filled with what he might do under his Christmas tree.

"I'll leave the door unlocked," he whispered.

Tiny Tim could bless everyone if he wanted; Stella blessed jet lag. It meant she only received a short inquest following Linus's departure. Her mother wanted to know why she hadn't mentioned Linus before while her father treated her to another lecture on focus. Finally, they declared themselves exhausted and, after thanking her for a wonderful Christmas dinner, headed to bed.

Stella waited until the light underneath their door disappeared before tiptoeing to the living room in her bare feet. Sneaking out of the apartment made her feel like a teenager, the illicitness adding an extra layer of excitement. She paused long enough to grab a small box from beneath the tree and then slipped out the door.

Just as Linus had promised, the door was unlocked. Linus's apartment was a mirror image of hers, only decorated with a more masculine taste. She stepped inside to find the apartment dark, except for the Christmas tree. The evergreen bathed the grays and blacks in red light. A fire crackled in the gas fireplace.

"Linus?"

"Merry Christmas, love."

His voice wrapped around her like a warm caress. Turning around, she saw him in the easy chair by the fire, his clothes shed in favor of his paisley robe. His bare chest looked pink by the light. Her fingers itched to comb through the exposed hair.

"Brought you something to unwrap," she said, holding up the package in her hand.

"Lucky me. I love unwrapping things."

"What a coincidence. So do I." Smiling, she swayed toward him, and climbed on the chair, one knee at a time. Reaching down, she gave the belt of the robe a tug. The silk half knot fell loose easily. "See?"

"I thought I was supposed to be doing the unwrapping?" Linus's voice was thick and heavy with promise. Stella melted a little more. Her breathing quickened as Linus slipped his hands beneath her skirt and brushed her skin. Slowly, lightly, his fingers skimmed upward. When he reached the apex, his eyes widened.

"Silly me," Stella said, leaning forward. "Looks like I forgot the wrapping paper."

They didn't talk after that.

CHAPTER TEN

LATER, THEY LAY beneath the Christmas tree, Stella resting on top of him, Linus's robe draped over her back like a blanket. She kissed the hollow of his throat, the taste of salt coming away on her lips. When she was in his arms, her parents, their expectations, the shadow of her insecurity, all faded away. In these moments she felt competent.

No, she felt special. Lucky.

Was this how his other lovers felt? Did he make the world disappear for them as well? The power he possessed frightened and amazed her.

"Penny for your thoughts?" Linus's voice vibrated in his chest.

"I'm thinking every Christmas should end this way."

"Naked and under a tree?"

"Mmm…" With limbs too boneless to move.

"I'll make a note for the future."

Only Stella wouldn't be here. She'd be in New York while he lay with someone else. She pushed the thought away. Thoughts of the future made her chest squeeze.

"I should go back soon," she said instead. "My parents will expect me in the apartment when they wake up."

"We still have time. There's no rush."

"If I stay here too long, I'll fall asleep."

"So?"

"So…" She lifted her head. "Your floor isn't as comfortable as a bed."

"Then we'll switch to my bed."

"Then I'll never leave."

"Damn, you've discovered my evil plan."

Stella yelped as he suddenly flipped their positions. Their bodies aligned naturally, her legs parting as he settled between them.

"I guess a few more minutes won't hurt," she managed to say, just before his mouth claimed hers. As always happened, she lost herself in the kiss.

Linus was in the process of kissing his way down her sternum when a flash of red caught her eye. Largely because her back was arched. It was enough, however, to bring her back to the present. "Your present. I forgot all about it."

"I thought I already opened my present. In fact, I was thinking of opening it again." He tried to resume his kissing.

Stella gave him a playful shove. "Your real present, silly. I dropped the box by the chair when we were otherwise occupied. I want you to open it before I leave."

Ignoring his exaggerated sigh, she scrambled out of his arms to retrieve the package. As she turned around, she caught him staring at her. "What?"

"You're beautiful," he said.

"I'm a mess." Her hair was tussled. Her makeup had to be smudged. And, she was kneeling bare-ass naked, her skin bathed in red Christmas lights.

"I happen to love messes," he said.

She looked at the box in her hands. A figure of speech. He didn't actually mean the words. They weren't... Well, they just weren't.

"Here." She held the box. "I know we didn't discuss getting presents, but..."

"Wouldn't feel right not to exchange gifts on Christmas," he finished.

"Precisely. Go ahead. Open it." She held her breath as he peeled off the paper. It had taken hours of web surfing and inner debate before she found what she hoped was an appropriate gift. Something of substance. Not too personal. Not too impersonal.

"A Swiss watch."

"A scientist's watch. At least that's what the ad said. It's antimagnetic. Durable, too. We'll have to see, since I dropped the box on the carpet."

Linus took the watch from the box and ran his fingers across the face. The shadows made his face unreadable.

"Do you like it?" she asked.

"It's...lovely."

"I'm glad." Her shoulders relaxed. "There's a note, too. At the bottom of the box."

Writing the note had been more agonizing than picking out the gift. She'd wanted to write something poignant like "certain memories last forever" or "you are timeless," but everything she came up with sounded too intimate or trite. She'd finally settled on simple.

"'To the best friend and neighbor a girl could have. Merry Christmas, Stella and Toffee.'" Linus looked up.

"Figured it was only appropriate her name be included."

"Of course. Wouldn't be right to exclude the cause of our friendship."

Stella got an uneasy feeling. Linus was saying all the right words. His response, though, felt off. Like she'd messed up somehow.

She'd spent too much time with her parents. They always exacerbated her insecurity.

"I believe I promised you a present, too." Linus set the watch aside and reached under the tree, the light dancing off his skin. And he thought her beautiful? He took her breath away.

She watched as he picked up a narrow gold box only to pause and set it aside in favor of a brightly wrapped square. "I hope you like it."

It was a silver bracelet with a tiny silver cat charm. Stella held up the charm so she could watch it sparkle. "Was Toffee involved in this gift, too?" she teased.

"I thought it the appropriate choice."

"I love it."

"I'm glad."

Again, he said the right words, but she swore his eyes weren't sparkling as brightly as before. There was a serious edge to his expression as he searched her face. Before she could ask why however, his hands were cradling her face. Her eyes fluttered shut, and once more, she lost herself in his kiss.

The day after New Year's, Teddy showed for what had become his monthly oversight meeting. Having officially challenged the will, he was now mandating them. Stella made a point of staying out of the matter. As she told Linus, while she loved Toffee and her job, she considered the inheritance battle a family matter. On the plus side, the situation served as a good reminder that the apartment and her position were only temporary. There were times when she felt entirely too at home.

"I understand there was an auction planned. That the estate was planning to liquidate some of Aunt Agnes's belongings," Teddy said when Mrs. Churchill answered the door. Since the incident in Berkshire, he'd dispensed with congenialities.

"Happy New Year to you as well," Stella replied. "How was your holiday?"

Teddy shed his overcoat and handed it over to the housekeeper, along with a request for tea. "My holiday was fine. I see you embraced the Christmas spirit," he said, taking in the greenery.

"Toffee and I did indeed. We had a wonderful holiday." If you called four days of trying to impress her parents and failing wonderful. She was beginning to wonder if she'd ever win their approval. There were bright spots, though. Like Christmas night. She fingered the silver charm dangling from her wrist. That weird moment under the tree, she'd decided, was simply leftover neuroses from being with her parents.

Teddy helped himself to a seat on the sofa, his arms stretched along the back as far as they could reach.

"I want to know about this auction. What were you planning to sell?"

Nothing anymore, thanks to his lawsuit. "The plan was to liquidate some unnecessary assets such as the wine collection and the art and furniture Agnes had in storage. The proceeds would have been reinvested and the interest added to the funds for Toffee's care. Obviously, the plan has been put on hold." Along with every other major financial decision.

"I should hope so," Teddy said. "That you would even consider selling assets without consulting me is appalling."

Stella settled in the chair across from him and dug her nails into the ends of the armrest. "It's the trust's job to decide what assets are sold. The only reason you are being given courtesy now is because of the lawsuit."

Apparently, she'd given up congenialities as well. "But if it makes you feel better, I can assure you we weren't selecting items willy-nilly."

"Now you aren't selecting items at all, are you?" Teddy replied.

"No. We are not." In football, they would call that a blocked kick.

Satisfied he'd gotten the last word on the subject, Teddy smiled. "Peter also tells me there's to be a museum exhibit. A retrospective of my aunt's career."

Peter had been chatty. "Yes. I've been talking to the V&A about it. Dame Agnes was an English institution. I have a meeting with the museum director next week."

"I would like to attend as well," Teddy told her.

"You would?" She didn't know why she was surprised, what with Teddy's increased scrutiny.

"My aunt had a lot of idiosyncrasies. As her only living relative, it's my duty to ensure that the narrative surrounding her life is told in a manner equating to her stature."

Bull. This was another ploy for control. Stella suppressed an eye roll. If only Linus were here. She could picture him giving Teddy the side eye. He had this way of arching his brow just so. Never failed to make her giggle. The man made everything more enjoyable.

Even something like New Year's dinner with his sister and her fiancé. A smile threatened as she recalled the mischief they'd gotten into hiding in the coatroom. Happy New Year indeed.

She'd hated sending him to work this morning. Forty-eight straight hours together and there she was practically begging for him to come back tonight.

She was definitely getting too comfortable.

"What is that?" Teddy interrupted her thoughts by pointing to the dining room table behind her where stacks of paper littered the surface. A disorganized outline of her novel. The past week had found her working on the novel more and more. Something about the project called to her. Jotting down notes and cross-referencing anecdotes with history reminded her of when she was young. She was ten years old and daydreaming again.

She doubted Teddy would approve, though. He'd want to review the narrative. No way.

"Here's your tea, Mr. Moreland." With exquisite timing, Mrs. Churchill came down the hall carrying a cup and saucer. "Black rooibos, two sugars, no milk. Just the way you like it," she said. "Oh, and I found this in the kitchen."

Using her free hand, she held up a gold-and-silver egg. "Looks like someone's been poking around the library desk again," Mrs. Churchill said.

Stella sighed. "Put it on the mantel, please. She hasn't been able to get up there since I moved the chairs."

"Is that Aunt Agnes's kaleidoscope?" Teddy snatched the egg from the housekeeper's hand, teacup rattling from the motion. "Are you telling me you let the cat bat this around like a common cat toy?"

"I didn't let Toffee do anything. She's was being a cat. They get into things and cause mischief."

"Not if they're being properly watched."

This time she did roll her eyes. "Clearly you've never owned a pet."

"If I did, I wouldn't let it crawl all over the furniture messing with valuable items. I'd pay closer attention."

How dare he? The man comes in and starts throwing his weight around, doesn't bother to ask about Toffee—doesn't even say her name—and now suggests she wasn't keeping a close enough eye on her cat? "I keep a very close eye on Toffee, thank you very much." Rising from her seat, she crossed the room and snatched the kaleidoscope from Teddy's hand. "I know everything there is to know about that cat. Where she sleeps, what cat food flavors she likes best. I even know what kind of brush she prefers. Don't tell me I'm not paying attention." She ended by gently setting the egg on the mantel, beneath Agnes's portrait. The gold's shine looked brighter behind the evergreen needles.

"Obviously you weren't paying attention when she decided to play with the kaleidoscope."

"In Miss Russo's defense," Mrs. Churchill said, "the creature causes most of her trouble in the middle of the night. Hard to watch her at two in the mornin'."

"Then she should be crated overnight," Teddy replied. "I'm not going to see a valuable object broken because of a cat's curiosity."

Stella's eyes widened. "Did you seriously suggest I put my cat in a crate? No wonder Agnes didn't make you Toffee's guardian."

"She's not your cat," Teddy replied. "You are

the cat's caretaker, and to be honest, I'm not sure you're doing as good a job as you should be."

He joined her at the mantel. Picking up the kaleidoscope, he turned the egg back and forth in his fingers. "First you left her unattended in Berkshire, and now this."

"I left her with you."

Teddy ignored her. "Who knows what's been broken or lost on your watch."

"Nothing," she replied, snatching the kaleidoscope back.

"All the same, I would like to see that inventory you were working on. To ascertain for myself."

Stella's stomach dropped. There were still a large number of items unaccounted for. The trust had hired an investigator to look into the situation, but so far, no luck. While the disappearances predated her arrival, Teddy would still take issue.

"Of course," she said. "I'll need a few days to pull together all the information. There are a number of files to be merged." She also needed to talk with the trust advisers before handing over anything.

"Next week will be fine. I'm nothing if not flexible. Although I'm warning you. If I detect any kind of subterfuge or an attempt to delay hoping I'll forget the request, I'll have your job. Do I make myself clear?"

The threat came on a cloud of tea and peppermint so strong it made her want to gag.

"Crystal," she replied.

And to think, when she first met the man, she'd thought him a pompous buffoon. The thought that he could ruin her reputation—and being sacked for mismanaging the estate would definitely ruin her reputation—made her stomach churn more.

She needed to call Linus. She needed his levelheaded way of telling her everything would be all right.

She needed him.

"It's going to be fine, you know," Linus said when they went to bed that night. "You have done an amazing job of taking care of Toffee."

"I think you're a wee bit biased, but thank you anyway." She kissed his cheek. Just as she knew he would, he spoke to her common sense. The missing items weren't her fault. In fact, talking with Teddy might actually answer some of her questions.

The man beside her yawned. "Sorry," he said. "I'm getting old. Can't stay up the way I used to."

"Then go to sleep. We'll talk in the morning."

"Mmm… Sounds perfect." Rolling onto his side, he pulled her close. Big spoon to her little one. "G'night, love," he slurred.

"Good night, old man." She smiled to herself before scooting backward until the space between them disappeared completely. His arms were the perfect cocoons. She closed her eyes and listened to Linus's breathing. He made her feel so safe and secure. Special.

What would she do without him?

You'd better learn. You're out of here in six months.

Stella's eyes flew open, her heart suddenly racing. The antsy sensation she'd felt at Christmas returned, only tenfold. She understood why now. She was getting way too attached. Her casual affair was playing much too large a role in her life. Everything she did, everything she thought revolved around this man.

At least a half dozen times a day she had to stop herself from texting about some random idea or occurrence, and when he texted her? It was like sunshine wrapped in the ding of her phone. And on the few nights he didn't sleep over, she would toss and turn all night for the emptiness in her bed and wonder if the separation caused his chest to ache, too.

No wonder her heart was racing. She was digging herself a hole she did not need.

There was only one solution—expand her world beyond Linus. Of course he played a central role in her life. How often did she see anyone else? Maybe if she saw other people, Linus's presence wouldn't have such a pull.

There was a man at the auction house with whom she'd had several meetings. Niles Brown. He'd invited her to dinner at their last meeting, but she'd said no because she had to get home to feed Toffee. Tomorrow, she would give Niles a call, see if he wanted to grab coffee.

She tamped down the guilt in her stomach. It was just coffee. She was increasing her circle of friends. And even if it was more than coffee, she and Linus weren't in a committed relationship. What they had was casual, fun and noncommittal. Linus knew that, same as he knew he was free to go out for coffee with a friend, too. It was no big deal.

She continued arguing the point with herself for the rest of the sleepless night.

"You're going out to dinner," Linus said. "With another man."

"You say it like I'm planning to commit murder," Stella replied. "We were originally going to have coffee, but Niles's schedule got messed up, so we decided to do dinner instead."

"I see."

He looked her up and down. She was dressed in a black dress and pointy heels. Pretty fancy.

Oh, but what did he know? They were only friends and neighbors, right?

The phrase had been eating at him since Christmas night. And now she was going out with some bloke from an auction house he'd never heard her mention before.

The worst part was he couldn't say anything, not really, because he'd arrived at the same time as Teddy Moreland. The older man was standing by the fireplace waiting on Stella's inventory report.

He leaned against a sideboard, attempting a casual veneer. "I didn't realize you'd become friends with anyone at the auction house."

"Yes, well…" She smoothed her beaded necklace against her throat. "I thought it a good idea to expand my social circle. I mean, I've been monopolizing your time since I arrived."

"Did I say I minded?"

"No, but that doesn't mean it's fair. Especially since we're not, well, you know."

In a real relationship. "So you're doing this for my benefit? Is that what you're saying?"

"Yes. I mean, no." She began fiddling with her necklace again. "I just think it would be a good idea if I spent time with more people than just you and your family."

"Right. Where is he taking you?"

"A restaurant in Soho. He didn't say." That explained the dress.

"Soho has some lovely places." He'd been planning to take her to one of his favorites for Valentine's Day.

"You're okay with my going, then?"

No, he wasn't okay, but what good would saying so do? "Are you asking my permission?"

"Of course not. I… Never mind."

"Excuse me for interrupting such an important conversation." His expression anything but sorry, Teddy strolled toward them, hands stuffed in the pockets of his overcoat. "I don't have all evening. You called and said the inventory list was ready?"

"On the dining room table," Stella said. "Hold on."

While Stella went to retrieve the paperwork, the old man smirked at Linus. "Trouble in paradise, Collier?"

Linus would be damned before admitting anything to Moreland. "How are things, Teddy? Still fighting to prove you're better than a cat?"

"I don't have to prove anything. I'm confident things will work out in my favor."

"You know what they say about overconfidence, Teddy. It often clashes with reality."

"We'll have to wait and see about that, won't we," Teddy replied, his smirk widening. His cocksureness set the hair on the back of Linus's neck on edge. The man was up to something.

"Here you go, Teddy." Stella returned carrying

a thick manila envelope. "If you have any questions, call."

"Don't worry, I will," Teddy replied. "Have questions, that is. Nice to see you again, Collier."

"Still upset about what happened in Berkshire, isn't he?" Linus remarked, once Teddy closed the door. "Man knows how to hold a grudge."

"I'm still not one hundred percent certain he was telling the truth about what happened that night," Stella said. "You can't tell me he wouldn't have been happy if Toffee disappeared into those woods."

Linus was prone to agree. While he figured Agnes had her reasons for disinheriting Teddy, he largely thought the man was a harmless, drunken blowhard. Then again, eleven million could turn even a harmless blowhard nasty.

"I still don't think you have anything to worry about as far as your job is concerned. Teddy's interested in the money, not being a guardian."

"Maybe, but a guardian controls the money and Toffee's life span." She looked over to the terrace door, where Toffee lay on her side. Seeing the worry in Stella's profile, the lines that deepened by her mouth, the forlornness that clouded her eyes, Linus's first instinct was to wrap her in his arms. He couldn't, though. If he did, he would end up kissing her senseless, and he was no longer sure that's what she wanted. From him, anyway.

"I should be leaving," he said. "Your company will be here soon."

"You don't have to leave," Stella said.

"Don't you think having your FWB around might make things awkward for your date?"

FWB. Friend with benefits. The term sounded sour on his tongue.

"Will I see you tomorrow?"

He had his hand on the doorknob when she asked. "I don't know," he said, keeping his eyes on the brass knob. "Thomas wants to start discussing our summer product line. There's a good chance I'll be tied up all week."

"Oh."

She sounded disappointed. "These things happen."

"I know. I… It'll be strange not seeing you, is all."

"I'm sure if you get bored, your friend Niles can entertain you." Immediately, he regretted the childish remark. To make amends, he turned and offered her a half smile. "Have a nice time at dinner."

CHAPTER ELEVEN

"KEEPING IT CASUAL. Nothing will change. I'm going to dinner with some bloke from work." Scotch splashed the sides of his glass as he waved his arms widely. He was on his second Scotch and probably his second mile of pacing the living room.

How could Stella go on a date with someone else? Sorry, dinner. It was ludicrous. They were sleeping together, for God's sake. Had been for months. Didn't that mean anything?

Not for friends with benefits, it didn't. The two of them were neighbors. They were keeping things casual.

Casual, casual, casual. He was going to strangle the next person who said the word.

He should have kissed her like he wanted to. Grabbed her and kissed her until she forgot all about what's his name.

He should have told her he didn't want her seeing anyone else, because… Because…

Suddenly the emotion that had been squeezing his chest for months had a name. "I love you," he whispered, the words loud in the silence. He loved her. The more he repeated the words, the more certain he became. He, Linus Collier, had fallen in love with the American next door.

And she didn't love him back.

Christ. He plopped down on his sofa. When irony hit, it hit hard, didn't it?

Appeared he'd finally learned what it was like to be just another shag. Was this how his former lovers felt? As if someone had plunged a knife in the center of their chests? He owed them all apologies, because damn, it hurt like hell.

"You made your point, universe. You finally doled out your punishment." He emptied his glass. That was the universe's ultimate punishment.

Just then he heard the elevator doors. Leaping up, Linus hurried to the front door. This was what his life had become. Standing with his ear pressed to a door trying to eavesdrop. On the other side were muffled voices. Stella and her date. He heard Stella's keys. Imagined her opening the door, then leaning in for a good-night kiss. Linus squeezed the tumbler. That should be his good-night kiss. He should be leaning against her door frame waiting for an invitation to come inside.

So help him, if she invited what's his name inside...

She didn't. The elevator doors dinged, telling him as much. Linus breathed a sigh of relief, because he wasn't sure how he would have ended the thought.

What did he do now?

Talk to her, you idiot. Tell her how you feel.

If she knew how important she was to him—that he bloody loved her—then she'd realize this whole "casual lovers" thing was ridiculous.

In the back of his mind, he wondered if he should wait until he had a clear head, but he pushed the thought aside and headed outside. He needed to talk with her tonight. Otherwise, it would eat at him all night long. Besides, he was declaring his love, not picking a fight.

Now that he'd had a moment to get used to the idea, he was gobsmacked. Never in his life had he expected that he, Linus Collier, would fall in love and want to commit to a woman. Guess there was more of his father in him than he realized.

Stella answered the door in her stocking feet. Since the summer, her hair had grown so that the bob skimmed the center of her neck. Tonight she wore her hair pulled back in a hairband to better show off her heart-shaped face. As happened whenever he saw her, she took his breath away.

"Linus, what are you…?"

He didn't let her finish. Cradling her cheeks, he kissed her deeply. Instead of smiling her hands clutched at his shirt as she kissed him back.

"Bet you didn't kiss him like that," he rasped when the kiss ended.

Her brows drew together as she stood a step back and stared at him. "Were you spying on us?"

"Don't be sound so surprised. I live next door. Did you think I wouldn't notice when you came home?"

"That is possessive and creepy."

"Are you serious? After I let you go out with another man?"

Stella glared at him. "You didn't let me do anything."

"You asked for my permission."

"Hardly. I was keeping you informed out of courtesy. You didn't have a say in it one way or another."

The conversation wasn't going how he planned. Stella stomped away from him, into the living room, where she stopped in front of the fireplace. Toffee's portrait stared down on them while the original wove around his legs. At least someone in the house was glad to see him. Linus obliged the cat and gathered her in his arms.

"I'm sorry," he said. "You're right. I don't own you and I shouldn't have implied that I did."

"Thank you," she said. "Now, why are you here?"

"Because I..." *I love you.* Suddenly he was afraid to say the words. "I wanted to see how the evening went. Did you have a good time?"

"Seriously?"

"Yes, I want to know. I'm curious." She continued giving him a skeptical look. "All right," he said after a few moments. "I'm jealous."

Stella blinked. "You are?"

"Does that surprise you? We *are* sleeping together. I'm not one for sharing."

"Is that so?"

Terrific. She thought him possessive again. Closing his eyes, he out a long breath. Everything was coming out wrong. They shouldn't be fighting.

Still holding Toffee, he turned and put some space between them. There was a cat perch near the terrace doors. He placed Toffee on the top level, then stared at their reflection in the glass. Behind him, Stella could be seen playing with the armchair piping.

If this was going to work, he needed stop dancing around the words and tell her how he felt. "I know that night in Avebury, we said we would keep things light and noncommittal." He refused to say that horrid word. "But I don't think I can. I hated thinking of you being out with someone else tonight. Absolutely hated it."

As he spoke, he watched her reflection. Thus far, she hadn't stopped studying the chair. "What are you saying?" she asked.

"I don't want us to see other people. What we're doing isn't a low-key thing for me anymore." He spun around. It was important she see his face. See his sincerity when he bared his soul. "I love you."

"Wh-what?"

He smiled at her stunned expression. "I don't blame you for being shocked. I was shocked too when I realized it."

"You're drunk."

"No. I'm completely clearheaded right now, and I mean every word. I love you and I want us to be together."

Unable to stay separated a moment longer, he took her in his arms. "You're trembling." Like a leaf in a cold wind. He tightened his embrace.

"I… I can't believe it," she said. "You can't be in love with me."

"But I am."

"You don't understand." She pulled away, leaving his arms empty. "I mean you can't be in love with me."

Linus looked like she'd slapped him. "What the bloody hell is that supposed to mean?"

"It means we had an agreement. We were going to keep this—us—casual." For some reason, he grimaced when she said the word. "I have plans," she said. "In New York."

"You're not in New York now. You're in London."

"I know where I am," she snapped. What mattered wasn't where she was, but where she was going. "My point is that I'm leaving in a few months."

"So?"

"So, I don't have time to fall in love." Unable to face him and continue this argument, she headed to the mantel. "When I return home, I need to give one hundred percent of my attention to building a career in finance."

"Right. Just like your father wants. So he can brag about you to the relatives."

"I'm not doing it so he can brag." It was a good thing she'd turned her back to him. Kept her from snarling in his face. "This is about me, and proving that I'm—"

"As good as your siblings. You shouldn't have to prove anything."

Stella shook her head. He didn't understand. Not really. How could he? He'd spent his life accepted. The born scientist, his role in the family predetermined, what did he have to prove?

Linus's hands came to rest on her shoulders. Without looking, she knew his expression was marked by softness, his eyes compassionate and heavy lidded. "I don't care what you do or who you are," he said. "I just want to love you."

And she wanted his love. Oh, but she wanted it. She closed her eyes. Her limbs were shaking. Just like that day on Fifty-Second Street, she was afraid to move. It was like she was holding on to a ledge by her fingertips. If she let go…

You'll be happy.

You'll forever be a disappointment.

Her heart twisted in her chest. "I can't…"

"There's nothing more to be said, then, is there?"

His hands slipped away, leaving her standing by the fire, cold and alone, listening to his footsteps grow fainter.

"Linus, wait!"

She turned just as he reached the door. "I…" The words wouldn't come. Not the ones he wanted to hear. They remained trapped in her chest, blocked by fear. "I'm sorry."

She could see the disappointment in his eyes from across the room. The sorrow reached across the distance and pierced her heart, where, she suspected, it would stay for a long time. "So am I," he said. "I'd hoped… Never mind. Doesn't matter now. Goodbye, Stella."

Goodbye? Was this it? She stumbled a few steps forward, only to stop and collapse on the sofa. From out of nowhere, Toffee leaped on the cushion beside her, meowing softly. "It's for the best," Stella told her. "We were getting too attached."

Forty-eight hours later, there was still a persistent lump in Stella's throat that had her constantly feeling on the verge of tears.

Thing was, crying would be welcome. Only she couldn't. God knew she'd wanted to since Linus walked out the door, but tears refused to come. It was as if her body wanted to hold on to the sadness.

I'll be fine in a few more days.

That had become her new mantra. She'd been repeating the words all morning. When she woke up in her empty bed. When she found Linus's T-shirt in her laundry hamper. When she heard the elevator door sound as Linus left for work.

I'll be fine in a few days.

This heavy, pervasive sadness was a normal reaction to the ending of a friendship. And that's all it was—a friendship. A friendship with good sex.

Make that great sex. Not to mention being the best friendship she'd ever had.

Dammit! Why did Linus have to spoil everything by saying he loved her? Didn't he realize that if she let her feelings go beyond casual she would be forced to rethink…?

No, she wasn't going down that road. She had to return to New York and focus on her career as expected. That was what she wanted.

"You understand, don't you, Toffee? I have to prove myself."

Toffee didn't answer. The Angora had her back to Stella and was bathing. She hadn't slept on the bed the past two nights, either. A paranoid person would think the cat was trying to punish her.

She'd come around. Eventually the cat would need her chin scratched and Stella would once again be her best friend. In the meantime, she had a meeting to prepare for. The accountant was coming by to discuss the yearly expense budget.

Numbers work was exactly what Stella needed. Forty-five minutes later, she was properly immersed in figures when there was a knock on the door. Stella's breath caught. He'd come back.

"I'll get it, Mrs. Churchill!"

She hurried to the foyer, pausing to check her reflection in the mirror. Her face was peaked and her hair flat, but otherwise, she was presentable. She brushed the bangs from her face and, taking a deep breath, opened the door.

It was Teddy Moreland.

He wasn't alone, either. Peter Singh was with him as well as another man she didn't recognize. "Hello, Stella," Peter said. His dour expression clashed with his red cashmere scarf.

Seeing the three men together set Stella's nerves on edge. She and Peter always met at his office. "Is something wrong?"

"I'll say there is." Teddy pushed the door wider and barged inside. "I need you out of my apartment."

"Your apartment?" Stella squinted at the man in confusion.

Peter took a deep breath. "Teddy. We agreed that I would handle the situation."

"What situation?" Stella asked.

"Let's sit down, shall we?" Peter said. He and the other man stepped into the living room. Teddy was already there, still wearing his overcoat and pacing in front of the fireplace. The other men shed their overcoats and draped them over the back of the sofa before making themselves comfortable.

Stella opted to stand. She had a very bad feeling. "Would someone please tell me what's going on?" she asked.

Peter started. "Stella, this is Montgomery Armstrong."

"My attorney," Teddy stated.

"Nice to meet you." It wasn't really, but she didn't know what else to say.

"I'm afraid this isn't a social call," Armstrong replied. "My client has come to me with some very disturbing concerns about the estate and your management."

"What do you mean?" Stella asked.

"It means you're a thief," Teddy said.

"Teddy, we agreed."

"Well, she is."

A thief? Stella decided to sit down after all. "I

don't understand. Is this about the discrepancies in the inventory I gave Teddy? I've already told Peter about that. We've asked an investigator to look into the matter."

"Yes, I know," Armstrong said.

"Then what is the issue? Did the investigator find something?" And if so, what did his finding have to do with her?

"Stella, it appears—"

"What are you tiptoeing around for?" Teddy stopped his pacing to glare at her. "The truth is that those items were never missing. You only said they were so you could sell them online."

"What?" He was drunk; he had to be. "That's ridiculous."

"Is it? I first got suspicious when I discovered a crystal figurine missing following your visit to the country house. At the time I thought I was imagining things, but then I read your inventory report and saw how many items you claimed couldn't be accounted for, so out of curiosity, I decided to do a little investigating on the internet. Lo and behold, I found the very same crystal figurine being offered on an auction site."

Upon finishing, he smirked like a detective having announced the killer in the drawing room mystery.

Feeling very much like an accused killer, Stella glared daggers at him. "I didn't steal anything,"

she said. If anyone was guilty of helping themselves at Agnes's country house, it was him, the
miserable liar. He was the one spending his weekends there.

She turned her attention to Peter. "Are you certain it's the same figurine?"

"Yes." Reaching into the briefcase he'd brought
with him, the lawyer removed a tablet. "The same
account was auctioning off several other items
that have been listed as missing as well."

"And you think I'm the one responsible?"

She wasn't sure if she should scream or be sick
to her stomach. How could they possibly think
she would do something so blatantly dishonest?
Teddy seemed awfully confident, though. Taking the tablet from Peter's hand, she studied the
contents. Sure enough, there were Agnes's belongings, on a page registered to a user named
Expat92.

"I had my tech people track the account," Armstrong said. "It's registered in your name."

"But that's impossible! I didn't open any account. I didn't steal anything." Stunned, she
looked at the tablet screen again. The auction
page listed a dozen items, all objects she'd listed
as missing, including the crystal cat figurine. All
posed in front of a backdrop of gray linen and described as having been owned by the late Dame
Agnes Moreland.

This was a nightmare. "I didn't do this," she said.

"Then how do you explain the site being registered in your name?"

"I… I don't know." Teddy had set her up somehow. Paid a hacker or something. Why, she wasn't sure. Yet. "But it's not my account. Why would I be so stupid as to sell items from the very estate I'm managing, and such benign items at that? A figurine? Garnet earrings?"

"Obviously you figured the smaller objects wouldn't attract attention," Teddy said.

"He's right," Peter said. "A few trinkets in an estate this size wouldn't be missed."

Panic started rising in her throat. Her innocence wasn't going to be enough to acquit her; she needed proof.

If only Linus were here with her. His faith in her would have given her confidence. He always believed in her.

Linus wasn't here, though, so she had to go it alone. She looked down at the tablet screen. The first item for bidding was Agnes's monogrammed lighter, which, Stella knew from reading, she had bought herself after getting her first acting paycheck. The auction had both the dates and the history incorrect.

"Here," she said, showing the tablet to Peter. "Read the description. It's incorrect. Wouldn't I list the correct anecdote?"

"Not if you were looking to deflect?" Teddy was smirking again, like the cat who had eaten the canary. Stella did her best to ignore him.

"And where would I take the photos or store the objects? They aren't here in the apartment. Go ahead and search—you won't find them."

"Of course we won't. You're not that foolish," Teddy said.

Thanks for the credit. Apparently, she was only slightly foolish—enough to post the items in the first place. "You won't find photos on my computer or phone, either."

"Photos can be deleted," Armstrong said. "I'm sure if we had an expert check, we would find—"

"Nothing," Stella snapped. "You would find nothing." If they thought she was taking this lying down, they were sorely mistaken. This was her reputation they were defaming. She would fight them tooth and nail.

Her phone lay on dining room table where she'd been working. "Here," she said, practically throwing it at Teddy's attorney. "Let your experts have at it. They only thing they'll find are photos of London and Etonia Toffee Pudding." And a few photos of Linus. If they deleted any of those, there would be hell to pay.

"Do you think us so naive that we don't realize you could have used a second phone?"

Stella let out a frustrated scream.

"Is everything all right?" Mrs. Churchill came running down the hall from the kitchen. "It sounded like someone stepped on the cat."

"Everything is fine," Stella replied.

"Speaking of Etonia Toffee Pudding, where is she?" Armstrong asked.

"Sleeping in the guest bedroom, like she has the past two days," Stella replied. "Why? Are you afraid I tried to sell her, too?"

"No, but Mr. Moreland has also voiced concerns about her level of care."

"What? Her care is fine."

The doorbell rang. Probably the police, arriving at Teddy's helpful suggestion, since he seemed determined to have her carted away.

"I've got it," Mrs. Churchill told her.

Meanwhile, Stella attempted to stare down Teddy's attorney despite the man's unimpressed demeanor. "I treat that cat as if she were my own pet. No, better than my own pet. I treat her like a bloody masterpiece."

"Exactly the way Dame Agnes would have wanted," a familiar voice added. Stella's insides swooped at the sound. What was he doing here?

Linus stood next to Mrs. Churchill, looking gorgeous in a navy blue suit. In a gathering of four men, his vitality dominated the room. Stella's insides ached with the desire to disappear into the safety of his embrace.

"I heard you scream and was concerned," he said. "What's this about Toffee's care?"

"Who are you?" Armstrong asked.

"Linus Collier. I own the apartment next door. Dame Agnes was a very good friend of mine, and I can vouch that Miss Russo here has taken extraordinary care of Toffee." Stella gave him a grateful smile.

"Is that so?" Tilting his head, Teddy's lawyer fixed his attention on Linus. There was a hint of satisfaction to his expression. Her brother used to make the same face when they were younger, at awards ceremonies. It was the look of a person who believed they had a win in their pocket. What had Teddy told him?

"My client has mentioned a pair of incidents that has left him concerned," the man said as he pulled a notebook from his briefcase. "He believes Miss Russo isn't paying close enough attention to Etonia Toffee Pudding. There was an incident in Berkshire where the cat nearly escaped into the woods."

"Because he didn't latch the terrace door properly! I wasn't even there."

"Exactly my point," Teddy replied. "I watched her the entire day. You were clearly too busy looking for objects you could steal."

"I did not…"

"Stealing? What are you talking about?" Linus

looked back and forth among Armstrong, Teddy and her. "And I was with Toffee as well that afternoon. We spent time with her together, at least when you were awake and not sleeping off the gin and tonics. Miss Russo is correct," he told Armstrong. "The cat escaped because after the backdraft, the terrace door failed to latch. If anyone failed to keep a close eye on Toffee, it was Teddy here. I asked him to watch the cat while Miss Russo and I took a dinner break."

"Proving my point," Teddy said. "You were neglecting her."

"Oh, come on. If I wanted to neglect the cat, would I have brought her with me to Berkshire? She was with me precisely because I didn't want to leave her alone." What next? Stella wondered. Suggesting she left the terrace door open on purpose?

Meanwhile, confusion continued to mark Linus's features. "What was all this about stealing?" he asked.

"Teddy thinks I'm selling Dame Agnes's belongings online," Stella told him.

His face went from confused to appalled before she could blink. "That's ridiculous. Those items were missing before you even arrived."

Stella very nearly cried. Even after she rejected him, he still believed in her. What had she done to deserve him in her life? "I've been trying to tell them, but apparently the online account is in my name."

"Accounts can be falsified. May I see?" She handed him the tablet.

"We've had experts verify the account," Armstrong said. Peter nodded in confirmation.

While Linus looked at the tablet, Stella returned to the more recent questions. "You said there were a pair of incidents."

"Mr. Moreland found the cat playing with a valuable heirloom."

"You did no such thing, you big blowhard." At Mrs. Churchill's retort, the group leaned back in surprise. Apparently, after years of waiting on him, the housekeeper had decided not to hold back any punches.

"I'm the one who found the 'heirloom' on the floor in the kitchen. I also found a pen cap, a pencil and a pair of ear swabs from the jar in the guest bathroom. Quite the little devil at night, that one is. We were always finding things in strange places. Once Miss Moreland and I caught her batting around a diamond drop earring after Miss Moreland left them on the dresser."

"Come to think of it, she was fond of my son's bouncy balls when we had her at our house," Peter said.

"Proving my point that the cat should be secured at night, so that she doesn't hurt herself or break something of great value."

"You mean stick Toffee in a crate," Stella said. "She owns the freaking house!"

Teddy looked down his nose. "For the time being. The courts may decide differently, and if that's the case, I don't want to risk losing something of import because the cat is running amok."

"As far as I'm concerned," Armstrong added, "Mr. Moreland has raised a number of adequate concerns, not the least of which is the evidence of criminal activity. Therefore, we request that Miss Russo be removed as manager of this estate."

CHAPTER TWELVE

STELLA SANK INTO a seat. She wished she could say she was surprised, but she'd been expecting the request since they sat down. She'd failed. At a job simple enough to do in her sleep. When the numbness wore off, she was going to be sick to her stomach. What did she do now?

Armstrong wasn't finished. "It's clear the cat should be watched by someone with a vested interest in her health and welfare as well as the future of the estate. We're going to petition that Mr. Moreland be named temporary guardian until a ruling on his lawsuit is issued."

There it was. Stella had been wondering about Teddy's endgame. It was control over the estate. If she was named unfit, and he got temporary guardianship, he could then try to maneuver his way into a permanent guardianship if he lost his case. Either way, he had control over Agnes's money. The bastard.

Poor Toffee. She would be locked in a crate at bedtime and/or ignored for the remainder of her life. This would be as good a time as any to muster up the ability to cry.

"I have a couple questions," Linus said. His face was still focused on the tablet. "Did you track the IP location for the user?"

"We did. It led to the coffee shop around the corner," Armstrong told him.

"Did you check the security tapes?"

The lawyer smiled. "This isn't *CSI*, Mr. Collier. Not every business in London has security cameras."

"Too bad. The time stamp says the photos were unloaded around forty-eight hours ago. Stella wasn't home."

"No kidding," Teddy said. "She was—"

Linus cut him off. Seemed everyone was done with Teddy. "No, I meant she was out for the evening on a…date. Look." He showed Stella the first auction item. "Unless I'm mistaken, you were out for dinner at that time."

Sure enough; the auction was listed as starting at 7:00 p.m. "Teddy must have heard me talking about meeting Niles for coffee." Clearly missing the section of the conversation where they'd switched to dinner.

"I'm sure he'll be able to vouch for you, and you know I will." His smile was tinged with sadness.

"No one said she did the posting on her own. She could have easily hired someone." Being as close as he was to his payday, Teddy wasn't giving up.

"Who would I hire?" Stella asked. She knew, maybe, a half dozen people in the city.

Teddy pointed to Linus. "Him. The two of you are sleeping together, aren't you?"

Stella watched as Linus drew himself up to his full height. With slow, even strides he crossed the room to the mantel where Teddy stood. The older man's body shrank in on itself in the face of Linus's towering presence.

"Did you just accuse a member of one of London's wealthiest and most established families of selling stolen items over the internet? My family was doing business with the royal family before your first ancestor wielded his first coal shovel. We have never, ever been associated with illegal activity. If you're going to toss out those kinds of accusations, you better be ready to back them up in court."

"Men have done worse for the woman they're sleeping with."

If looks could kill, Teddy would be dead on the spot. Linus's voice, however, remained calm and controlled. "Hate to break it to you, old boy, but Stella and I are nothing more than friends."

One at a time, his words landed hard in her stomach. How she wished she could cry.

Since she couldn't, she channeled her energy into one last question. One she wanted to hear Teddy try to answer. "Why would I sell Agnes's belongings so blatantly anyway and risk being fired? Over what amounts to a few trinkets. I need this job and Peter's good reference for when I return to New York. Getting fired would ruin my life."

"She's right," Linus said. "If anyone has anything to gain from all this it's you, Moreland. Have you searched his property?" he asked Armstrong. "Checked his computer?"

"How dare you!" Teddy said, glaring. "I would never steal Aunt Agnes's belongings. She was precious to me."

"Little defensive, aren't we, Teddy? And let's be honest. Agnes disliked you intensely."

If it weren't such a dire situation, Stella would have laughed out loud. The sparkle in Linus's eyes reminded her of the day they met. Seeing it eased the tightness in her chest. He made even bad situations tolerable. "Mr. Collier makes a good point."

For the first time in a while, Peter Singh made himself known. He stood up and smoothed the front of his suit coat. "I think, in the spirit of due diligence, we should investigate Mr. Moreland's computer and phone along with Miss Russo's. After all, we don't want to make any false assumptions."

"Feel free to investigate mine as well."

"We appreciate the cooperation, Mr. Collier."

Teddy looked about to have a spasm of some

kind. His eyes were huge and his spine rigid with tension. When Peter made his request, he'd blanched and clenched his fists.

"This is an outrage," he said. "I refuse to be a victim of a witch hunt."

"You started the witch hunt," Stella said. "If they're going to search my belongings, then they are damn well going to search yours as well."

"What's the matter Teddy? You don't have something to hide, do you?" Linus asked.

"My client will be happy to cooperate," Armstrong said. "He has nothing to hide."

Based on the rattled look in Teddy's eyes, Stella wasn't so sure. It was clear he'd counted on her being so shaken by the evidence that she wouldn't put up a fight.

The meeting ended with her agreeing they could take her laptop and phone for examination. Linus insisted on having his company lawyer present for when they examined both his and her electronics. To protect their interests, he explained.

"Thank you," she said once the trio had left. Armstrong had made a point of saying she would be closely monitored until the issue was resolved. Mrs. Churchill had gone as well.

"Silly to have separate lawyers when one will suffice, and he's on retainer," Linus replied.

"I meant for defending me." That he believed in

her innocence unconditionally meant a lot. "Especially after the other day."

He shrugged. "Our personal issues don't change the truth. You're an honest, good person. What shocks me is that I had no idea the lengths Teddy would go to, to get control of the money. He must have been planning this for a while. Since before Agnes died."

"Money makes people do crazy things. Agnes must have told him the terms of the will and he figured he needed a backup plan. Or two. Makes you wonder what he'll try to do next."

"With luck, nothing. They'll trace this little scheme back to him and that'll be the end."

"What if they don't? What if he's covered his ass?" Granted, he looked terrified at having his electronics searched, but Stella had already made the mistake of underestimating the man once. She didn't want to make the mistake again.

"They'll find something. His witch-hunt bluster was the last stand of a man who knew he was in trouble."

"I hope you're right."

"I am, and if I'm not, my lawyer will make his life such a living hell that Teddy will wish he'd never thought of the idea." His smile came and went in a flash. "Don't worry. You'll head back to New York with your glowing reference as planned."

"You needn't sound sarcastic."

"My apologies. I'll keep the bitterness at bay next time."

"Linus…"

"I'm sorry," he said, gaze dropping to the floor. "I'm being childish. You're right. There's no need for sarcasm, especially when your livelihood is at stake."

"Thank you." She dropped onto the sofa next to him. Now that the immediate threat was gone, exhaustion replaced the adrenaline in her system, and all the feelings she'd been keeping at bay washed over her. Once more she longed to fall into his arms.

"I've missed you," she said.

"I've missed you, too."

What she really wanted to say was that she'd had a giant hole inside her since he walked out, that without him she'd been empty and alone, but she was too afraid to say the words. She let her body do the talking instead, her fingers shaking as they touched the back of his hand.

A soft sigh escaped Linus's lips. "Stella." Longing laced his whisper. "Don't."

"Why not?" she asked. Why ignore the need they felt for one another? Their bodies were made to be together. She kissed the corner of his mouth, then kissed the other corner. Over and over, butterfly kisses that moved to the middle until his lips parted. "Why should we be lonely when we work so well together?" she whispered against his lips.

As much as it killed him, Linus pulled away from her. "Because I want more," he said. "I want more than sex and passion in the moment. I want you."

"You have me," Stella said.

"Do I?" He had her body, yes, but he wanted all of her. Her heart and soul. "I want your love."

"I already told you, I can't love you."

"You keep saying that word. I can't love you. You can't love me. Like we would be breaking some kind of rule by having feelings for one another." He wasn't asking if she could love him; he wanted to know if she did.

"Oh, Linus." She flung herself backward, her head falling back against the sofa, and covered her eyes with her hands. "What good would saying *I love you* do? It wouldn't change anything. I would still have to go to New York."

Slowly, she let her palms slide down her face. When she lifted her head, he saw pleading in her eyes. "Can't we just leave things the way they are rather than invite a whole lot of pain?"

But he was already in pain. Payback for Victoria and every other heart he ever broke. That he was getting what he deserved didn't make the

pain easier to swallow. Neither did the desperation in Stella's eyes. "What good would it do?"
he replied. "How about the fact that we could be
happy? We could build a life together. One that
you actually want instead of a career to appease
your father's ego."

"My father's ego has nothing to do this." Even
as she argued, Linus could see she didn't believe
what she was saying. "This is about me going
back and proving I'm not a delicate, anxiety-rid-
den flower who can't handle the pressure."

"Bull." The word came out harshly, but Linus
didn't care. He was angry now. Two minutes earlier, Stella had all but admitted she loved him,
only to run away. "At least be honest with yourself. You want your father's approval. You want
him to tell you that you're as good your brother
and sister."

"Is that so wrong?"

"It is if it's never going to happen." Her father's
approval might as well be a cat toy on a string.
"There will always be another goal, another sibling accomplishment to best. You're going to be
spending your entire life running a race you can't
win."

Stella stared at him, eyes shining. "Are you
saying I'm not good enough, too?"

"Of course not!" He kicked himself. "I think
you're bloody marvelous. I'm saying no matter

what you do, it won't be good enough for your father."

"You don't know that."

"Yes, I do!" Knew it in his gut and she did, too. Problem was, she blamed herself rather than the man truly at fault.

Washing a hand over his features, he paused and looked her in the eye. "It's not your job to fulfill your father's dreams."

Stella shook her head. "You don't understand."

"Yes, I do. I watched my sister, Susan, beat herself up for years because she didn't think she measured up. I watched Victoria—"

"I'm not Victoria," she snapped.

"I know," he snapped back. Their stories weren't remotely the same—he realized that now. The dissimilarities didn't stop him from fearing she would fall into a dark abyss, though.

Their argument was going off the rails. He could argue with Stella until he lost his voice, but she had already made up her mind.

The most maddening part? He would give up everything and go to New York with her if he thought that was what would make her happy.

"Do you even want to work in finance? At Mitchum, Baker?" he asked.

As he expected, she scowled in response. "Of course I do. I worked my ass off to get that job." The ends of her hair moved back and forth as she shook her head. "I don't understand why you're doing this. You know how badly I need to go back and prove myself."

"There you go again. You *need* to go back. You *can't stay* in London. What do you want, Stella? Do you really want a lifetime of seventy-hour weeks and working Christmas? Or do you want to be happy?"

"What makes you think I won't be happy?"

"Because you bloody froze in the street going to work, that's why. Happy people don't freak out on the way to work."

He'd gone too far. Anger flashed in her eyes. "I think you should leave," she said. "Check that. I *want* you to leave. Who do you think you are telling me what I want and don't want? What I do with my life is my business. I choose my path. Not you. Not my father. Me."

And the choice she made didn't include Linus. "Fine." He wasn't about to beg any further. "Go ahead and choose. But ask yourself this. Why did you freeze in the street that day? Was it really burnout or were you trying to get off the path?"

For the second time in forty-eight hours, he walked away.

Luck was on Stella's side—in terms of work, that was. The outside expert was able to prove her computer was not the computer used to create the auction account. Linus's lawyers delivered the news a few days after Teddy's visit. Apparently that was how they were going to communicate from now on—through third parties. The lawyer also told her that the expert traced the account back to a bartender who worked at a pub near Teddy's house. He also revealed that Teddy paid him to set up the account, citing technical ineptitude. Poor guy had no idea Teddy was scheming to get custody of Toffee.

When confronted with the evidence, Teddy naturally proclaimed his innocence and blamed Stella. At least he did until they found the crystal cat figurine wrapped in a swath of gray linen in his flat. Then he proclaimed righteous indignation over being cheated out of what he considered his rightful inheritance. In the end, to avoid scandal, he agreed to withdraw his challenge. Whether he would succeed Toffee as the heir, Stella didn't know. Since the cat would survive for years after Stella left town, it didn't really matter.

She hadn't seen Linus since he walked out of her apartment the month before. Nor had she cried. At least the lump in her throat felt smaller, and she wasn't chanting "this will pass" as often. Probably because she was furious. As badly as she missed him, she wanted to spit in his face. How dared he presume what she wanted or judge her rationale? If he cared at all, he'd support her decisions, not tell her to chuck everything so she could stay in London and work on Agnes's biography.

"You understand, don't you, Agnes?"

From her spot over the mantel, the actress gave her an imperious stare. Stella had discovered an old journal of Agnes's at the bottom of a box of books. Reading it gave deeper resonance to all the artifacts she'd collected. Dame Agnes had been as ambitious as she'd been beautiful, and as such, she'd ruthlessly pursued her career. The men she knew were divided into two groups: Casual Lovers and Men Who Could Aid Her Career. Stella added a third category, which she called Unfulfilled Suitors. They were men who showered Dame Agnes with gifts but got nowhere. Dame Agnes didn't have room for foolish romantics.

Dame Agnes spent the last years of her life with a cat for a best friend.

Stella didn't want to think about that.

Instead, she decided to go for a run. The weather outside was rainy and cold, but she didn't care. The fresh air would clear her head so she could work.

She got as far as the elevator when Linus's door opened. Holding her breath, she turned expecting to see his blue-gray eyes.

"Sorry." Susan Collier gave a wave. "Just me.

Linus is in Scotland for a few weeks. He asked me to water his plants."

"Oh," Stella replied. "I didn't realize."

"I figured."

The two of them shuffled from foot to foot while waiting for the elevator to arrive.

"Started wedding planning yet?" Stella asked after a moment. She thought about mentioning her breakup—*was* it a breakup if you weren't dating?—but if Susan was watering the plants, she probably already knew.

"A little," Susan replied. "We're thinking of a Christmas wedding. The holidays are a bit of a thing in our family."

"So Linus said. That sounds nice. You can do a lot with a holiday theme."

"I think so. Lewis doesn't really care. He said he'd be happy eloping, but I want the wedding. Call me vain, but I like showing off my handsome fiancé."

"At least he's willing to indulge you. Means he respects your choices."

"More like he knows how good he looks in a tuxedo," Susan said. "I'm not the only one who likes showing Lewis off. Lewis likes showing off Lewis, too."

The elevator bell dinged, and the doors parted. As they boarded, Stella suppressed a smile. Susan and Lewis were forever teasing one another. Reminded her of how she and Linus would banter back and forth.

Her stomach grew heavy. Seemed to grow heavy a lot lately. Such as whenever she thought of Linus. The night before she'd been watching a movie when the actor playing the lead turned his profile to the camera. The man's nose and cheekbones looked so much like Linus's she had to turn off the television.

Susan was staring at her. Linus's sister had a way of looking at a person and reading their thoughts. She had to be getting a hell of a reading right now.

"You must hate me," Stella said.

Susan shook her head. "Don't be ridiculous. I understand where you're coming from. I think you're wrong, but I understand."

There were days when Stella wasn't sure she understood herself. "May I ask you a question?" she asked.

"Sure," the youngest Collier replied. "Can't guarantee I'll have an answer, though. What do you want to know?"

"Well…" She hoped the question wasn't too prying. "Linus mentioned that when you were growing up, you struggled with being different from Thomas and him."

"Not exactly. More like I struggled with not being as perfect. I don't know if you've noticed, but Linus looks like an underwear model. Thomas is worse."

Stella blushed. She had noticed. "Must have been hard growing up in their shadows."

"Try impossible," Susan told her. "I spent the better part of my teens and twenties feeling like the dumpy, ugly stepsister."

"I'm sorry." Stella took a long look at the woman. Linus's sister was on the thick side, but she carried herself with such confidence and pride, it was impossible to see her as anything but beautiful. What had changed?

"Simple," Susan replied, when Stella asked. "I met Lewis." The doors opened to the lobby. "He made me realize that I was special in my own unique way, and that it was okay if I wasn't tall, dark and handsome like the other two. Why do you ask?"

"No reason." The awkwardness of the lie was made worse by Susan's knowing look. "I was curious is all."

"It also helped that my mother moved to Australia to be part of a reality show. She was the chief reason I felt inferior. But you know all about that."

"What do you mean?"

"Your dad," Susan said. "Linus told me how you're under pressure to be successful. Relax," she added when Stella's shoulders went back.

"He only mentioned it because he thought I might have insights. I didn't, by the way."

Having reached the first floor, they stepped out into the lobby. "I told Linus everyone needs to work out their issues at their own pace. You can't force someone to change their behavior just because you want them to."

"Thank you. I appreciate the vote of confidence," Stella said. A little too late to bring her and Linus back together, but it was nice to know she had an ally.

"No problem," Susan replied. "According to my brothers, sharing my opinion is one of my strong suits." Flashing a grin, she headed toward the front door. Stella followed and was heading down the building steps when Susan turned around.

"One more thing," she said, "because that's who I am. Something I learned from Lewis this past year. When you feel like you can't compete, you can either stay in the race and struggle, or you can find a race you like better."

A taxi pulled up and she slid inside, leaving Stella alone to ponder her comment.

CHAPTER THIRTEEN

Spring

"WHAT IS GOING on with you?" Thomas asked. Seated at the head of the conference room table, his brother stared at him over the frames of his new reading glasses. "Florence tells me you forgot the Paris teleconference?"

"I didn't forget," Linus said. "I wrote down the wrong date. There's a difference."

"Barely. I had to spend twenty minutes explaining to Philippe d'Usay that we weren't purposely wasting his time."

"I'm sorry. I'll send him an email and apologize."

As he typed a reminder note in his phone, Linus could feel his brother's eyes on him. "I don't understand," Thomas said. "You've always been slightly on your own planet, but you've been more distracted than ever these past few months. Half the time, I don't know where your head is at."

"People confuse dates all the time. It's hardly a major crime," Linus replied.

"I know what's bothering him." The comment

came from Susan, who sat at the table across from him. Thomas's version of a family intervention. "Stella's leaving in a few weeks. I take it the two of you still aren't talking?"

"Stella broke up with me, remember?" Not that it stopped him from staring at her door every day debating whether he should knock.

"I'm sorry. I really hoped after she and I talked in the elevator that Stella would come around."

"I know you did," Linus said, "but I'm learning some baggage is simply too heavy to throw off." She loved her father; she was afraid to admit she loved Linus. It was too big a hill to surmount. He simply had to accept that she was leaving.

"Just so we're clear, this is Stella your neighbor we're talking about. The one we helped out this winter." Thomas looked between the two of them. "Is she the woman you were talking about at Christmas? The one who wanted to keep things casual?"

"One and the same," Linus replied.

"Only Linus didn't want to keep things casual," Susan said, "so they broke up."

"I'll be. Where the hell was I during all this?"

"Running a company and raising a family," Linus said. "I figured you had enough on your plate."

The comment earned him a serious glare. "You

should know better than that. We're family. I always have time for you."

"Maybe I wasn't in the mood to share. The only reason Susan knows is because she's nosy."

It was a testament to how miserable he must look that Susan didn't protest.

The seriousness of Thomas's expression softened into one of brotherly affection. "I'm sorry. I wondered when we talked at Christmastime, but I hadn't realized how serious your feelings were."

"Surprise!" Linus faked a smile. "They crept up on me as well. Doesn't matter, though. The lady has commitment issues." Along with daddy issues and self-worth issues.

And now she was leaving in a few weeks, and he was wondering if he hadn't made a mistake by insisting that Stella declare her feelings.

"For what it's worth, I think she feels the same way you do," Susan said. "The expression on her face when I ran into the other day? She was crushed I wasn't you."

"She does feel the same way," Linus told her. He may be new at love, but he could see the emotion in Stella's eyes.

Her Christmas present, the real one, was in his nightstand, the package unopened, a new reminder of his past mistakes. Wasn't that always the way? He finally made peace with his guilt and remorse over Victoria, only to have new guilt and remorse.

"You know, she's not leaving just yet," Susan was saying. "There's still time to fix things. At the very least you can steal a few more weeks."

"I don't want just a few more weeks," Linus said. "I want forever. What?" Thomas and Susan were looking at him like he'd sprung a second head.

"Sorry," his brother said. "I'm still getting used to the idea of you wanting to settle down."

"You've got plenty of time. In case you weren't listening, the lady's moving back to New York."

"So?"

"So," Linus told him, "she'll be on the other side of the Atlantic."

"Last time I checked, we're a global economy. There's this thing called an airplane that will take you across the ocean. Our company owns one, as a matter of fact. There's no reason you can't continue long-distance or relocate yourself."

"If only it were that simple." Briefly, he explained what happened to Stella in New York and her need to win her father's approval. "I tried to convince her that it was a waste of time, but she wouldn't listen."

Again with the staring. "What now?" he asked them.

"Let me see if I understand," Thomas said.

"You tried to undo a lifetime of insecurities with one conversation, and when she didn't listen, you walked away?"

"What was I supposed to do?"

"Stick it out, you idiot," his brother said. "If you love her, it shouldn't matter if she's off chasing her father's dream or not. What matters is being there to support her and being there if she stumbles again."

Linus stared at his phone. Thomas was right. He'd been focused on making Stella love him on his terms and hadn't stopped to think how it would be for Stella to untangle her complicated family relationships. If he loved her, he needed to be willing to fight for her heart. "If I went to Manhattan, I would be leaving Colliers," he said.

"Most likely," Thomas said, "but I think we'll survive. What matters to Susan and me is that you're happy."

Stella made him happy. All he wanted in return was for her to find happiness, too, like she wished for in Avebury. If her happiness lay in New York City working seventy hours a week for Mitchum, Baker, then that's where he'd go, too.

Only question now was, would she let him?

"Did you talk to Mitchum, Baker and give them a return date?" Kevin Russo boomed over the phone in an effort to talk louder than the static. "You've only got a month."

"Yes," Stella replied, "and I know." To be precise, she had twenty-nine days.

She also had a headache. Nothing severe, but enough to leave her distracted and fuzzy headed. Talking to her father was the last thing she needed.

At least the weather was turning. Today was the first day of sun in weeks. Opening the terrace door, she stepped outside to see if reception would improve. After months of being trapped inside, it felt good to feel the sun on her skin. Below her, Belgravia waved hello. She was going to miss this view when she went home. She was going to miss a lot of things.

Stop thinking about him. Nearly four months and thoughts of Linus still plagued her.

Maybe if you told him you loved him, he'd still be around.

What good would it have done, though? Admitting her feelings would have only made saying goodbye harder.

Stella had long given up trying to figure out when she went from burying her feelings to admitting she loved the man. The words bubbled up one day and refused to be denied. Too bad she hadn't been able to say the words when they counted.

"Stella? Can you hear me?"

"Sorry, Dad. I went outside for a better signal. I was saying that they're installing the exhibit on Dame Agnes's life at the end of the month as well. I think I might stay an extra day to make sure everything goes all right."

"It's a museum exhibit. What could go wrong? You hang a picture in the wrong place?"

"It's a lot more complicated. You want the exhibit to—"

"Stella, honey, you finish the job on the thirty-first. You don't need to work for free, especially for a bunch of stuff from some actress's career."

"Dame Agnes wasn't just some actress, Dad."

"Regardless. You've had your leave of absence. Now it's time to come home and build something you can be proud of."

"I'm proud of this exhibit," she said. In fact, she was proud of everything she'd accomplished over the past eleven months. Maybe it wasn't a job at the top consulting firm in the world, but she'd tackled some pretty interesting projects and done a good job.

"Did I tell you that Joe is going to be lead counsel on this double murder trial in Chicago? City councilman's wife killed him and his mistress. It's going to be super high profile."

Good for Joe. Another legal feather in his cap full of feathers. The change of subject annoyed her more than usual. "Did you hear what I said, Dad?" she asked. "I said I was proud of this exhibit."

"I heard you. You're proud."

"Very," she said.

"I'm glad. You should be proud of a job well done, no matter how small it may be."

God, did he have to diminish everything? Her head throbbed in response. Slowly, she began to pace the terrace perimeter, using the click of her heels on the concrete as a kind of meditation metronome. With each step eastward, she tried to steady her breathing.

You'll be chasing forever. Linus's voice floated into her head. Was he right? Was she chasing something unobtainable? Ever since Linus said it, she'd been listening to her father's voice more carefully. Little by little she saw the pattern. No matter what she accomplished, her father wasn't impressed. Maybe it was because he disapproved of her having gone to London, and once she was back in New York, the negativity would ease up.

Would it?

There was one way to find out. She took a deep breath. "Can I ask you something, Dad?"

"Sure," he said. "What do you need?"

"Nothing. I was wondering what you'd think if I decided to write a book. About Dame Agnes."

She could tell from the silence on the other end

of the line that he didn't think much of the idea at all. "Why do you want to write a book about her?"

"Because she lived a fascinating life. You know how I've always liked history."

"Hey, you want to write a book on this woman, have at it. Personally, I would write a thriller or something that people might read. Always surprised me your brother didn't do something along those lines. You might decide the same thing once you're back in America."

"Actually…" Time for the test. "I was thinking of taking another year off. Peter Singh said I was welcome to stay here and keep an eye on Toffee in exchange for rent."

She wasn't really thinking of time off. Sure, she'd felt a thrill when Peter made his offer—her first thought being that she could rekindle her relationship with Linus—but she'd already made her plans. The only reason she was floating the idea now was to gauge her father's reaction.

There was more silence on her father's end of the line, followed by a loud, boisterous laugh. "That was a good one," he said. "You really had me until you got to pet sitting."

"It's not a joke, Dad. Peter really did offer me the penthouse so I could work on the novel."

"Yeah, but you're not seriously considering it, right? You already lost a year on this pet-sitting thing."

"Estate management, Dad." Did it really matter at this point? "And it's a tempting offer."

"I didn't spend all that money on your education so you could run away to Europe and pretend to be a novelist. It's embarrassing enough that you couldn't hack the pressure and had to take this leave of absence."

She didn't burn out to embarrass him. In fact, the opposite. She'd burned out trying not to embarrass him.

Interesting how either way it was about him. The fact she'd actually had a nervous breakdown didn't seem to matter.

Linus was right. "I'm never going to win with you, am I, Dad?" Not unless she was perfect, something she would never be. Eventually she'd stumble or fall short. It was inevitable.

"What are you talking about?"

"You're not going to be happy unless I'm a superstar like Camilla and Joe."

"Don't knock your siblings. Your sister and brother worked very hard to get where they are."

"Yeah, and I worked hard, too. I busted my ass in grad school and at Mitchum, Baker, and all you did was tell me how Camilla and Joe were doing better."

"That's because you needed the motivation. You always needed that extra push."

"No, Dad, I didn't. I was doing the best I could."

"You can always do better. I tell the same thing to Joe and Camilla. Never settle. That's always been your problem. You were willing to settle."

Stella shook her head. Her father couldn't see it, couldn't see the effort she put into trying to make him proud. That was because effort wasn't a tangible outcome. You couldn't brag about effort the way you could an award or accolade. Her father couldn't hold up effort as evidence of his success.

The question then was, did she really want to keep chasing what she could never catch, or did she want to chase something—and someone—that mattered?

Did she even still have someone to chase?

All this questioning was making her headache worse. She needed to lie down.

"I've got to go, Dad. I'll talk to you later."

Her father was in midsentence, but she didn't care. She hung up and headed back to the western end of the terrace.

"Hey, Toffee," she announced on her way inside. "You want to lie on the bed with me? I'll rub your belly."

The sofa where Toffee had been sleeping was empty. "Toffee?"

Suddenly, a horrible sense of déjà vu gripped her. She'd left the terrace door open. Rushing outside, she searched under every piece of furniture and anything else a cat might find interesting.

There was no sign of Toffee.

She was afraid to look down. From this far up, Toffee would look no different than a speck of garbage. A big, furry, flat speck of garbage.

Think positive, Stella. She hurried inside and across the hall.

Thankfully, Linus was home, and he answered the door. Stella didn't have time to register how surprised he looked, or how good. She rushed past him into his living room. "Toffee got out," she said. "I need to check your terrace."

Linus followed her outside, and together they searched the entire length. No Toffee.

Stella was going to be sick.

"Don't panic yet," Linus said. His hand rubbed gentle circles between her shoulder blades. How was it after all these weeks and all her rejection, he was still comforting her? "Did you check everywhere in the apartment?"

The apartment? "No. I saw the open door and assumed Toffee escaped." Stressed out as she was, she didn't think to look around the apartment.

There was gentleness to his smile that made her heart skip. "Then maybe we should check there before we assume the worst," he said.

He said *we*. "Thank you. I didn't mean to make you drop everything to help me."

"Don't apologize. I'll always be here if you need me."

If only he knew how wonderful those words made her feel. "I don't know what I'd do without you," she said. "Truly."

She didn't have time to examine the emotion that crossed his face before he'd taken her hand and led her back to her front door. "Let's go check your apartment," he said.

On the way, Stella crossed the fingers on her free hand and said a little prayer that her little Toffee Pudding had decided to hide in a bedroom instead of going outside.

Her prayer was answered sooner than she expected. As they walked into the apartment, they saw Mrs. Churchill standing in the living room holding a furry white bundle.

"Toffee!" Stella rushed to take the cat from the housekeeper's arms.

"Caught the little demon batting the bloody kaleidoscope around again," Mrs. Churchill said.

"Naughty kitty. You scared the daylights out of me." Ignoring the cat's struggle to escape, she buried her face in Toffee's fur.

Free from her charge, Mrs. Churchill closed the terrace door. "Can I ask you to keep the door closed? The breeze kicks up the dust."

Because dust. Stella couldn't help but smile at the request. "Absolutely, Mrs. Churchill. My apologies. Would you mind getting this little mischief maker a chicken treat? It's almost her snack time."

"Oh, sure. She causes trouble and we give her a treat. It's like Dame Agnes never left. Come on, you. Let's get you a chicken tender."

Once the housekeeper was down the hall, Stella turned to Linus. He looked so right standing in her living room, it hurt.

"Thank you," she said. "Seems like whenever I've got a problem, you show up to help me solve it."

"Everyone needs a wingman," he said with a grin. "I'm glad I was home."

"So am I."

Now that he was here, she didn't want him to leave. There was so much she wanted to say. Where did she begin?

Maybe with three simple words. Would that be enough? A lump rose in her throat.

"Linus, I…"

"Hold that thought."

He disappeared out the door, only to reappear holding a small package. "I'd planned to come by and give you this as soon as I worked up the nerve."

Taking the box from him, she studied the gold foil wrapping paper. The box looked vaguely familiar, but she wasn't sure why. "What is it?"

"Something for New York. Open it and I'll explain."

Her hands shook as she peeled off the paper.

Inside lay a gold necklace with a charm in the shape of a ribbon.

"It's to remind you of our night in Avebury. You wished for happiness."

"I remember." The lump in her throat had tripled, making the words hard to get out.

"I meant what I said that night. All I want is for you to be happy. And if going back to New York so you can prove yourself is what makes you happy, then I'll support you every step of the way." Lifting the necklace from the box, he stepped behind her to fasten it around her neck. "I love you, Stella," he whispered. "I'd rather support you in New York than live in London without you."

Had he said what she thought he said? Needing to see his expression, Stella whirled around. Eyes filled with love met hers.

"Do you mean it?" she asked.

"Every word."

The logjam in her chest broke open. Stella burst into tears. Deep, sobbing tears that wouldn't stop.

"Shh, it's okay, love," she heard Linus whisper.

The arms she'd been missing desperately wrapped around her. She collapsed against his chest and cried like she'd never cried before.

Linus loved her. He supported her, no matter what her choice. She didn't deserve him, and he loved her anyway.

How did she get so lucky?

When she could breathe again, she kissed him. Passion wasn't enough, though. She needed to speak the words.

And so, when they finally broke apart, she wiped the tears from her cheeks and began. "I lied," she said, earning a confused frown. "That night in Avebury. I didn't really wish for happiness. I my real wish was to know my heart's desire. I was afraid to admit it at the time, but I didn't know what I wanted to do with my life."

"All right."

"Don't back away. Let me finish." She gripped his hands to keep him close. "I still don't know what it is I want to do with my life. Part of me wants to go to New York, and part of me wants to stay here in London with you and Toffee. But as confused as I am, there is one thing I know for certain, and that's what you mean to me. I love you, Linus Collier. You are my heart's desire. Without you, nothing else matters."

"You have me, Stella Russo. Always."

Stella smiled. For the first time in her life, she didn't feel less than. She felt loved, unconditionally, and she loved back with the same ferocity. The rest of her life would sort itself out in good time. She'd already found success.

CHAPTER FOURTEEN

Summary...again...

"ARE YOU SURE about this?"

Stella stared at the terminal sign for a couple beats before smiling at the man on her right. "I need to," she said. "He and I need to talk face-to-face. Dr. Winslow says it's the only way I'll get closure."

"Well, I'm all for closure," Linus replied, "so long as you want it."

"I do."

For the past several weeks, she and her father had been emailing, a conversation begun after Stella sent him a long, soul-baring letter. At first, her father responded with anger, explaining as he always did that he only wanted what was best for her. Little by little, with Linus's support, Stella managed to tell him that she was going to live her own life, and if he didn't find her accomplishments bragworthy enough, that was his problem.

"He's not going to like your decision." He was referring to staying in London and writing a novel. Stella didn't know if being a writer was going to be her lifelong passion, but right now, she was enjoying Agnes's story too much to care.

She managed a shrug. It still hurt, knowing she'd never really have her father's approval, but she was learning to cope. Being loved for yourself made a lot of difference. For the first time in her life, she felt in control. She had a project she enjoyed and a man she adored. Not a day went by that she didn't fall deeper in love with Linus.

"With you by my side, I can handle anything," she told him.

Linus kissed her cheek. "Always, my love. Always."

"Then let's do this." She picked up the cat carrier that was by her feet. "Come on, Toffee. Sooner we get going, the sooner we can get home."

Although in all honesty, she thought, looking at Linus, she was already home.

* * * * *